THE HOLDING DEAL

JOHN HEFFRON

TABLE OF CONTENTS

CHAPTER ONE

IT HAPPENS EVERY DAY. You're watching TV, listening to the radio, looking through a magazine. Someone on the screen/airwaves/pages catches your attention, and the disbelief hits you again. It's the same question you ask yourself over and over: Why is that person famous? They suck at singing. They can't act. They can't do anything you couldn't do. And yet they're everywhere. Is it just the shallow society we live in? Actually, it's worse. Let me explain.

Sometime around the turn of the twentieth century, powerful people discovered that moving pictures could, and did, have an incredibly powerful influence on public opinion. The famous had minimal boundaries. Beloved stars smiled or flashed some cash, and they gained access to places ordinary members of the public didn't.

A shadow organization called the Craft Talent Agency was formed. Not by the government. You're delusional if you believe the government actually runs things. I'm talking about the real elite—the ones who call the shots. The CTA began to deliberately and systematically make people famous. Like the FBI, and later the CIA and the Office of Homeland Security, the CTA maneuvered in ways known only to the elite few. Hiding in plain view under a national spotlight was the ultimate cover. The more famous CTA made a person, the more control it had over them. As the incentives—awards, money, influence—grew, so did the employees' commitment to their benefactors.

The CTA turned an ordinary small-town girl into a gigantic star. She infiltrated the White House and took down two members of a sitting President and another member of his family. From the *inside*. During World War II, two prominent movie stars kept tabs on—and, when necessary, eliminated—Hollywood's Nazi sympathizers. A famous magician and escape artist traveled the world on celebrated public tours. He also visited local police stations, where he first encouraged officers to lock him up and then gathered intelligence on law-enforcement organizations across the globe. I could share hundreds more examples, but this isn't a history lesson. This is about me. So why don't we fast forward?

In the 1980s, the CTA began devising one of the most dastardly inventions this side of the nuclear bomb. Remember when a certain pay TV network featuring music videos became popular? And how parents predicted it would ruin kids' minds? Well, that was precisely what Vidxy was intended to do.

First it was the VidStars who became famous. The elite first used them for undercover operations. Remember Electric? The bombshell with legs for miles who you know as the face of Vidxy? Whose chart-topping "I Know You Don't Know Me" you still belt out when it comes on the oldies station? Let's just say video didn't kill the radio star. Electric did. With the headphone cord off her Walkman

Along came reality television. With the first big hit, the CTA made people famous practically overnight. It was like a puppy mill for low-level spies, and as a result we now have The Mile-High Man and the Wives of Liberty. The current recruits are the stars of YouTube. For the CTA, making people famous for no discernible reason has turned into an art.

After the talent gets that initial taste of fame, however, the CTA begins to collect its pound of flesh. The training starts. A person experiencing the first trappings of success is called into a pitch meeting. They think they're about to launch their career on their terms —that they're going to lay out exactly what their stardom will look like. Instead, they discover they're a pawn, they have no choice in the matter, and the money and fame that they've come to need as desperately as air and water can be obliterated in the blink of an eye if they fail to do as they're told. The holding deal trap has been sprung.

Their absence while training is explained with an

alibi. Entering rehab is the most common excuse offered because rehab supposedly cures anything. Divorce, addiction, exhaustion? Nothing rehab can't fix. In reality, operatives begin learning a specific skillset. Computer hacking, hand-to-hand combat, demolition, sniper training. Any number of the esoteric fields CTA might have a need for, operatives learn. Depending on their level of fame, their physical attributes, and their innate skills, they are taught Jason Bourne–level tactics, from basic brush passes and dead drops to intelligence gathering and bang-and-burns. The latter is a demolition and sabotage specialty that is precisely what it sounds like—blowing shit up and walking away. The instructors try to limit jumping from rooftop to rooftop, though. Mainly because union insurance sucks.

The more famous operatives become, the more skills they learn, and the more gigs they perform. Most are kept at a lower level of fame and are given only a single skillset or function. Think, opening acts for headliners or supporting actors who have familiar faces but whose IMDbs list obscure series you've never seen. Only those with an affinity for the work or a special aptitude are selected for more sophisticated gigs.

Likewise, some operatives' fame lasts longer than others. One-hit wonders and the like don't disappear because their talent dwindles. Usually it depends on what missions they get. The entire casts of shows like *Yours and Mine*, which ran for seven seasons, have simply fallen into obscurity. The lucky few, the smart ones who know how to keep their mouths shut, end up in Canada making sappy Christmas specials in August that air a dozen times between November and December. You don't see much else of them.

You might wonder why celebs would allow their fame to be strangled while their colleagues are chosen for the higher ranks of stardom. Truth is, they think they're special. Most never realize other operatives exist. Only a select few learn that there are others like themselves. How? I'll tell you.

A booker with a job to fill contacts CTA. The agency has many divisions—TV, film, music, literary—and represents numerous personalities available for gigs. The agency then checks with the operative's manager to see if they are available. Say a gig needs to happen in Tampa. Which singer/comedian/author can be in that city on the required date? The agency finds out by contacting numerous managers. Upon confirmation, the manager handles all the logistics.

Now keep in mind, the talent has to perform both their public gig, which serves as their cover, and their clandestine assignment. Ever wonder why you see a performer sweating before they even come onstage? That's not stage fright. Chances are pretty good they were doing something they dared not be caught doing fifteen minutes before the show.

Probably the biggest pain in the ass for operatives is the inability to travel with any cool spy gear. They end up being MacGyvers. I mean, it would undoubtedly be suspicious if TSA found a thermal reader that works through walls in the carry-on of a stand-up comedian.

~

IT WAS DOWN to two of us. Each set lasted twenty-five minutes. I was nervous as hell, my palms sweaty. I'd spent years of my life working toward this moment, and even though I had already earned my spot on the nationwide tour with the other four finalists, this was a critical performance for me. No way I'd be getting rich working for the producers of the show. Exposure —*career* makers like interviews and guest appearances on talk shows—would be the pot of gold at the end of the rainbow for me.

I tried not to look irritated with the fuss the makeup artist was making over me; she was just doing her job. The guy who was going to be our tour agent had convinced me that looking good on national television was critical. Hell, I'd let him talk me out of the hoodie, jeans, and sneakers I habitually wore for performances and into a button-down shirt, slacks, and blazer. I balked at the tie though. A man has to hold on to his principles.

I glanced down at my watch impatiently. Ten more minutes. Only ten minutes before I potentially said goodbye forever to performing in dives. Goodbye forever to bars like in *Roadhouse*, where you have to perform behind a screen of chicken wire because the audience tends to get rowdy. Nightclubs where you walk confidently onto stage, certain the monologue you prepared is funny as hell until the audience convinces you it sounded funnier when you wrote it. College campuses where the headliner falls so flat half the audience is gone and the ones left are pissed. Goodbye to nightmares. Confidence goes a long way for a comedian, but sometimes you're screwed no matter what you do.

The sound of applause brings me back to the present. I can hear the emcee introducing me and see the stage manager frantically motioning toward the stage. He puts his hand on my chest to stop me as the emcee drones on, and then he shoves me forward into the blazing lights of the stage.

"Ladies and gentlemen, Mr. Drew Roberts!" The emcee glad-hands me and drapes an arm over my shoulder as I turn to the auditorium. I try in vain to see the audience with eyes still adjusting from the dimmer backstage lighting. Though I can't distinguish them as individuals, I can hear them. I can feel them. Like a dose of adrenaline coursing through my body.

"GUYS, thank you so much for showing up. Very powerful move. You should feel good. You," I say, pointing to a man in front, "you put pants on." I turn to the opposite end of the stage. "You left your house. That's good. So if anybody ever told you that you make shitty decisions, I would like to validate you. In case you have never been validated."

When I perform, I talk with my whole body. Everything is in motion. I impart my energy to the audience. Most of all, I emphasize the funniest bits with hand gestures and facial expressions.

"I have been listening in the back, and you guys have been amazing. So I gotta tell you this. A week before I came, I was traveling with my family. So even if you guys choose not to laugh at me, I will welcome the silence."

"I travel 47 weeks out of the year, and before I came here, I decided to take a little weekend trip with my wife. So I took my family trip and then my wife and I did a private little yickity yuck-yuck, bum-bum ba bum-bum weekend.

"Played a little Sade." I see someone who clearly has no clue agreeing with me. "Oh, don't nod," I call him out. "You're in your early twenties. You know nothing about that type of music. '*Let me rub you up and down and* —.'" I look back at the guy. "Nah, it's written all over your face.

"So I thought it was going to be a fun, romantic, uh, sneak-a-Viagra type weekend. But apparently, we were getting together for my yearly performance review. She'd been keeping notes the entire year and decided to use this weekend to go over some issues. Even rented a small conference room at a shitty Holiday Inn and has the nerve to do that fake smile as she greets me."

I plaster a grin on my face and gesture to the space behind me. "'Hi, welcome, sit down. All right. Did you get your welcome packet? Perfect. Then let's start this presentation. Let's take a look at the first picture.'" I press an invisible remote. "Shunk shunk. 'That is an empty paper towel tube on the paper towel holder. That's been empty for two weeks. I know because I left it to see what you would do. The answer was nothing. And if you look closely, you can see the wet marks where you actually attempted to dry your hands on the empty tube, which baffles me on so many levels.

"'Let's continue. Next picture.' Shunk shunk. 'Last week's internet history. Let's discuss some of these stops later, if we could. All right, last picture.' Shunk shunk. 'It's a cereal box that's up in the cupboard. Funny thing about that cereal box? It's empty.

"'Now, I know we've been working on putting things away, so I don't want to discourage you from this behavior. But I'd like to invite my guest lecturer to come up here and show you the proper way to close the cereal box, because your fist-in-the-box technique will no longer cut it.

"This family trip was a tough one. I made the tactical error of telling my sixteen-year-old stepdaughter she could bring some friends with her. At one point during the trip, my wife goes, 'Drew, you just don't know how to talk to sixteen-year-old girls.' And I go, 'Yeah, and it would be really creepy if I were good at talking to sixteen-year-old girls. Let's say I was good at it. Wouldn't your follow up question be, 'Hey, how the fuck did you get so good at talking to high school kids?'

"The other thing I learned this trip is this: all you twenty-something guys who have put off turning into your father this long, let me tell you something. You're going to turn into that dude. And you're going to turn into that dude the night before you leave on family vacation. You'll remember how pissed off your dad looked the night before a road trip. You'll remember that poor guy's face, and you'll know. Because as a kid, you don't realize he just started some dumbass argument with your mom in another room. As a kid, you're wondering, 'Why are you so pissed? We're driving to Gatlinburg tomorrow. I'm probably going to buy a new knife once I hit Pigeon Forge. What could be bad about that?' But now you'll get that, as a truck driver, he was pissed he would spend his only two weeks off a year driving you someplace.

"I did this dad move. And it wasn't premeditated. It just came from nowhere. I was watching my stepdaughter and her friends unload the truck. And I start doing this." I snap my fingers in a staccato rhythm. "And my wife goes, 'What are you doing?' And I go," I say the next part like a cranky old man. "'This is the pace we should be fucking moving to!' Not this Snuffleupagus, *Chariots of Fire*, I-would-never-think-of-carrying-two-things-at-one-time, how-am-I-gonna-text-if-something's-in-this-hand bullshit.'

"It's amazing to me how I can ask my stepdaughter to do something—even a simple, small request—and my words skip her brain and immediately enter her nervous system as if I tasered her. She could be walking by, and I could say, 'Hey, will you throw this away?', and it's," I roll my eyes three times, convulse, and shriek, "'My whole day is *ruined*.'" I pause for effect and to catch my breath.

"But there's one situation from this trip with my wife, and I don't know if I'm going to apologize to her. She *wants* an apology, but I don't know if I'm going to give it to her. Because I acted like a guy would act, and I don't know if I should apologize for that. See my stepdaughter had this guy with her, and the dude walks like this," I slump my shoulders, trudging aggressively across the stage, a sullen look on my face. "Right? And I noticed that whenever he walked towards people, they would see that negative energy and kind of step," I do a subtly sideways shuffle, "to avoid it. Well, at one point during the trip, this kid's walking towards me, gets right about here." I hold my hand up four inches from my nose. "And all I say is 'Walk the fuck around me.' I didn't say it like a dick. I just said it matter of fact. 'Walk the fuck around me.'

"And my wife goes, 'Are you getting puffy chesty with a sixteen-year-old?' So I said, 'Yeah, in fact, I almost whipped it out and pissed right in front of him in case he's a visual learner.'

"But now I am starting to think about things. I'm in my forties. I don't have kids of my own, all right? The kids in my house were all drafted." I give the audience a big shit-eating grin.

"Right? I recruited nobody myself. They all kind of came in the trade. Even if I had a kid yesterday, at 42, by the time that little shit moves out of my house, I'll be 66. Two weeks later, *I'll* be moving in with *him*. Right now, if I'm being challenged by a sixteen-year-old, I know I've got a good eleven seconds of air in my lungs.

I could dump him on his head for all eleven seconds. At twelve, ah, then he owns me, right? But I'm going to make him fight for that eleven seconds.

"Except the older I get, the more I'll be at a disadvantage. I don't want to be some old dad and have my son just lay over me. He'd be like, 'Hey, I'm taking the car.' And I'd be like, 'No, you're not,' and he'd just kink up my air hose and steal the tennis balls off my walker.

"This trip was also a little bit more challenging. I have a brother-in-law, and I took his 6-year-old little girl with us. I know nothing about 6-year-olds. Here is what I learned . . . quick. When a 6-year-old girl stands like this," I strike a regal pose, my nose and chin up, one hand delicately on my waist, "some shit is gonna be shared. And if she is wearing a princess dress, you're in a lot more trouble. If she gets dressed up for the occasion, your ass is dead in the water, man.

"They're smart, too, like, three times a row she pulled this little trick on me. She would go, 'Hey, will you watch a movie with me?'

"I'd go, 'Sure, love to.' And then I'd sit down with her and in my brain, I'm thinking, *Please don't watch the same movie you keep watching. Am I gonna have to sit through this one again?* Forty-two minutes into the same movie, three times in a row, the same week, I had to pop out of whatever universe my brain went to, look around, and go, 'How long has she not been sitting with me?'"

"I have no idea when she got up and left! I have no time stamp when she took off. I'm just by myself with the sippy cup eating Goldfish, just singing to myself, 'I can show you the world.' Meanwhile, she's in another room with all the kids going, 'Yeah, just put a movie in front of him. He's good. I usually give him a beer and put him down around three. By the way, if he pees and makes it into the toilet, give him an M&M. That's how me and his mom's working on it, so it's good that way.'"

THERE'S a certain feeling I get when I really connect with an audience—an elation that's as hard to explain as it is recognizable to any performer. The crowd was still laughing and applauding for me as the emcee came back on stage, but that extraordinary zing that tells me I knocked them dead wasn't there. It was time to find out who'd won, and I'd come up short.

The emcee called the other remaining finalist out and then babbled on about the show for a few minutes, one arm around my shoulders, one around hers. He wasn't as funny as either of us, but he thought he was. "Tonight is the night, guys. All of America is watching you, and our viewers at home are voting right now. In just a few minutes, the judges will receive the tally, and one of you will be declared America's Funniest Comic!" He turns to face me and asks for the eleventh time in the past four weeks, "And how are you feeling right now, Drew?"

My ex-wife could have told him that the wide grin I

gave him was the one I put on when I was either terrified or pissed. He didn't have a clue. "I'm hanging in there!"

"Good! Good!" He clapped my shoulder and turned to Candace. "How about you Candace? How are you feeling?"

Candace had been one of the friendliest contestants from the start. Everybody's mom. She was the oldest in the group, and it was she who soothed the bruised egos and smoothed out the interpersonal conflicts. She'd been genuinely funny, even in our daily conversations—something I couldn't say about everyone in the group. For a bunch of comedians, we were a very diverse bunch personality-wise.

"Right now, I'm wishing this was all over. My nerves are jangling!" Her grin was charming and jarringly sincere, and I felt a surge of admiration for the slight, unassuming redhead. The competition between the five of us had been fierce, but Candace had somehow managed to remain unaffected by all the tension and the stress.

The emcee turned toward the camera again. "When we come back after these messages, I'll have the computer tally of your votes, and I'll announce which one of our two finalists you have selected as America's Funniest Comic!" His broad smile lasted until the 'on air' light changed color on the front of the camera, though he didn't drop to a complete deadpan. We had a live audience in front of us after all.

CANDACE WON. It was close, but that didn't take away the gut feeling that was telling me Candace had been the better comedian that night. The elation I should have been feeling just wasn't there. It only took a few minutes backstage for the rain to begin falling on my parade.

"Good luck, kid," the emcee said as he was unbuttoning his collar and removing his tie. His gofer handed him a bottle of water, and he took a deep swallow before shaking my hand. He gave me a searching look, as if deciding whether to reveal some dark secret. After a long pause, he spoke in a low voice.

"Don't let this go to your head, Drew. Make the best of the opportunity, but keep in mind that being in the top five finalists of this competition did not make you a star. You have a lot of work in front of you, and the public is a fickle mistress. Not many people manage to make a living in this business; even fewer manage to reach the top levels of the profession." He shook my hand once more, this time a little less enthusiastically. "I suspect you're about to find out for yourself, but I'm giving you advance warning, and you need to pay attention to what I'm saying. Nothing about this business is what it appears to be. Make the best of whatever comes your way." With that cryptic comment, he turned his back and walked away.

It wasn't the end of the world. The five of us would be going on a national tour. It was a paid gig; five months of buses, planes, and hotel rooms that would all look and feel the same. I wasn't elated, but I felt pretty good. I was suffering a lingering disappointment at not having won, but I also felt a growing sense of certainty that I was headed for bigger things.

CHAPTER TWO

THIS ISN'T QUITE what I expected.

To begin with, my manager, Todd Rainey, is sitting on his ass back at home collecting twenty percent of the measly five hundred bucks I'm paid every week. We have a tour manager, a slick blonde twenty-something named Arthur Duffy, who dresses like a *GQ* fashion plate and talks like the Stanford MBA he is, except when he's dealing with us on a one-on-one basis. Then he sounds a little more like your friendly neighborhood used car salesman. Jason Keene, my agent, who has even less to do than Todd does with this tour, spends all his time with his other CTA clients while Duffy handles his chores yet *still*, he collects his ten percent.

I talk to Todd on the telephone once a week, and he is giddy about my prospects (and his future commissions) after the tour is over.

"This is absolutely fantastic, Drew! You're doing

great. I'm getting offers left and right. Decent offers paying pretty decent money."

"That's not doing me any good right now, Todd. After you take your cut off the top, and Jason his, I can barely cover rent and utilities at the apartment I need to keep available for when I get back. I have less than a hundred bucks leftover to cover whatever the tour doesn't pay for. I'm dying here."

"I know it's hard right now, Drew, but buck up. In just a few months, things are going to be way better than they've been in a long time. You just have to be patient. I promise."

I can almost hear my teeth grinding. *Buck up.* Hell. He's probably sitting comfortably in the recliner in his LA living room, sipping on a decent single malt scotch while I'm wondering if I can spare a dollar for a soft drink when I get off the phone. That's another thing that's about to go by the wayside. My cell phone. I can't afford it anymore. I'm going to have to start using the landlines in my hotel rooms and hope the tour doesn't back charge the calls to me the way they did the minibar items I ate at the first hotel. I argued with Duffy for almost an hour about that, and he said he'd "look into" getting that changed. He either didn't "look into" it, or the powers that be didn't change it. I don't know which is the case. Duffy never said.

While Duffy has been useless except in organizing our travel arrangements and keeping us fed, he's at least giving me tapes of every show. I spend every spare minute going over those tapes, analyzing each comedian's bit. I'm not looking for new material. I don't want to be a copycat. What I'm looking for is technique. I've been doing this for a lot of years now, but it's amazing how much I can learn from even the worst of performances.

Candace is my favorite. I'm beginning to think she was born with her sense of comedic timing, but I'm determined to learn how to match her delivery. She really is something. The rapport she manages to establish with her audience is something else again. She makes it look so easy, but I'm here to tell you, it's not.

Matt, a 23-year-old Anglo and the third of the finalists, grew up in Spanish Harlem on Manhattan Island. His material is punchy, and he delivers it in the staccato rhythm of a machine gun. He's good, but he doesn't have a knack for recognizing the boundaries of his audience. His bit goes over well in cities like New York, LA, and Chicago, but he's a little too over-the-top in Birmingham, Dallas, and Albuquerque. He's teaching me what not to do.

Percy T, née Percival Thetford, from downtown Atlanta (when asked, he just says he's from Peachtree, wherever that is), appears to have studied the wild and crazy format for comedians and is a close cross of Bob Goldthwaite and Eddie Murphy. Percy is almost as unflappable as Candace, and no matter what happens on stage, he manages to look cool.

Bob Thomas, the last finalist, is from somewhere in the Midwest. I forget where. It took me a while to figure out who he reminded me of, and I had to go back a ways before I got it. His bits are reminiscent of Jack Benny's work. Total deadpan delivery, no matter what his subject is. Bob's only fault, as far as I see it, is that he tends to get too highbrow for today's audiences. He's a little too condescending at times, and he's way too political. I know politics and religion are the lifeblood of some comedians, but I try to shy away from those subjects. Don Rickles made a career of offending people, but I don't have that kind of juice, and I don't want it.

My material is unique. When I have a new idea or when I get one from somebody else, I don't mind making changes here and there, but for the most part I stick to my routine. It may be my ego talking, but I believe my material is funny. What I want to improve is the way I present it.

I study the tapes, making notes, going back repeatedly to catch some technique or refinement that I want to incorporate in my own bit. I'm exhausted, but I've been especially kind to the housekeepers, and as a result the little basket holding coffee packets, cream, and sugar is overflowing, so I have a steady supply of strong coffee to keep me going.

A knock at my door startles me. "Just a minute!" I'm just wearing jeans, a t-shirt, and socks, so I snatch up the button-down oxford I laid out for the next show and shrug into it before answering the door. It's Duffy.

"Got a minute Drew?" His face is wearing a wide plastic smile that doesn't touch his eyes, and I'm instantly wary.

"Sure, come on in. Make yourself at home."

Like I said before, this guy always looks like he's getting ready for a fashion shoot, every crease crisp and razor-sharp and not a hair out of place. I have no idea how he manages to sit down on the sofa without wrinkling his trousers, but he does.

"I was talking to Todd earlier, and he tells me you're having a little trouble making ends meet."

"That's kind of an understatement . . ."

"CTA pays me pretty well to make sure our performers aren't troubled with outside distractions on the tour. Is your financial . . . situation going to be a problem for you, Drew?"

"Honestly, things are getting pretty tight, Duffy. I'm still trying to recover from the surprise deductions from my first paycheck."

"Ah, yes. Well, that was specified in your contract . . ."

Yeah, in print so fine I had to go back and read it with a magnifying glass.

"That contract also specifies that you can't take on outside employment for the duration of the tour, but I do know a way you can pick up some extra cash."

"I'm all ears."

"I'd have to know whether you're able to keep a confidence, Drew. This would have to be handled with the utmost discretion. If it turned out that you were unable to keep your mouth shut about this, there would be serious consequences. The least of which would be getting expelled from the tour."

"I won't deny that I could really use some cash. Who do I have to kill?"

"It's nothing that drastic, Drew."

"A joke, Duffy. Comedian here."

He doesn't even comment on that, just keeps going. "CTA needs little chores done. Say, delivering a sealed envelope to a specific person, or passing a message to a contact. For reasons that don't concern you, these chores must not be linked back to the agency in any way."

"It concerns me if this is anything illegal. I'm not getting involved with drugs, that's for damn sure."

Giving credit where credit is due, Duffy doesn't bat an eye. "You can rest assured we're not asking you to do anything illegal. The agency has perfectly legitimate reasons for maintaining their anonymity in these matters. I'm not at liberty to disclose the principals involved, but for these clients, discretion is of the utmost importance. I can't stress that enough. I can tell you, however, that if you and I come to an understanding, you will be subjected to a series of tests before you're assigned a real-world task."

"And the money?"

"You will be paid on the successful completion of each test, initially."

He has my attention for sure. "How much are we talking here, Duffy?"

He's grinning at me now. "Let's just say we're talking in multiples of your weekly paycheck and leave it at that for now."

I'm ready to shake hands with him. If he's on the level, and there's nothing illegal about what he wants me to do, I'm in. I'm not sure what he means about tests, but it sounds harmless. And if it's not something I'm comfortable with, I'll back out. Easy as that. I think I'm smart enough to be able to tell if he's asking me to do something shady. Besides, the agency is too big and too public to risk doing something illegal. They didn't become the largest talent agency in the world by being dumb.

"Okay, Duffy. I'm in."

CHAPTER THREE

DALLAS, TEXAS

"IT'S amazing how much technology has changed just in my short existence, right? It's pretty amazing. I was telling my stepdaughter how for a big chunk of my life growing up, we didn't have a garage door opener. She goes, 'Well, how did you guys get the garage opened?' A legitimate question if your reality included a garage door opener.

"So I told her what would happen. Your dad would pull into the driveway, sit there, and go—" I lift my arm, pull it back, then point forward violently.

"Then you would have to run out of the back and get underneath that door. Remember that?" I do my impersonation of a garage door rumbling down its tracks. "And no matter what, an animal would run out. 'I didn't know the cat was in the garage!' But he always was.

"I hated closing it because one, my vertical jump

sucked back then, and two, I had to reach the rope in cut offs way up here." I gesture to the tops of my thighs. "Remember how your mom would do them? 'Really mom? You're going with the Village People look?' Your pockets hung out on both sides and your white socks reached your knees, your comb tucked in there in case you wanted to feather your hair at any point during the day.

"But finally the door would come down. Your dad would always yell, 'Don't fuckin' slam it!'" I shake my head. "Once it starts going down, there is nothing I can do about it!

"But technology is crazy. I mean, I remember when we first got cable, there was a cord hooked up to the remote. And still you had to go—" I lean forward and punch my thumb hard at the imaginary button.

"Life went from a cord being hooked to the remote control to a remote-control car roving Mars. They're controlling that signal from Earth to Mars. Everything works. The signal comes back. Nobody really gives a shit. Everyone's like, 'Why wouldn't the signal work?'

"But that also amazes me because I have a wireless printer this fucking close to my computer," I move my hand a few inches from my side, "and there seems to be a problem every time I try to print. That signal has to travel maybe five, six inches? But it's too much, right? The signal gets weak and drops out right about here," I say, gesturing between me and the fake printer. "No idea why, it's just too far. Might as well be ten lightyears away. Then you get times like the other day, when my printer starts going off even though I'm not printing anything. So I look and out pops my 2002 tax return. I guess I owe the State of Nebraska some money."

"But it's crazy how technology changes. Like, I have so much music on my phone that I don't even know who sings it because I didn't have to do the work to figure out who the group is. I just go to this app, hold up my phone, hit a button, and it snags that song out of the air. Bam! I've got it. Some of you will never have to experience the embarrassment that used to come with tracking down a song. You'd hear a song on the radio, and you wouldn't catch the name of the artist. So you'd have to go to the mall, right? Maybe stop in at Chess King or Merry Go Round real quick. Oak Tree. Buy some Cavariccis. Maybe get a Japanese bandanna and tie it around your ankle." That gets a laugh.

"Get some parachute pants. Have a breakdancing competition later in the day." I bust out some dance moves. "*Sha-do do do do.*

"But eventually, you'd have to walk into the record store. You'd go up to the front counter guy. And then you'd have to sing that shit to that guy. Even if he obviously knew the song. You'd go, 'Hey, what's up? Do you got that song everybody's playing right now?'

"'What song is it?'"

I break out the dance moves again as I belt out the lyrics. "'Ain't nothin' gonna break-a my stride. Nobody gonna slow me down, oh no!'

"Even if he knows it, he's like 'Nah, not sure. Maybe you want to keep going?'"

"YOU REALLY WOWED THEM TONIGHT!"

"Thanks, Candace. I wasn't sure I was going to be able to get them going at all."

"Matt should've known better. This is Texas for God's sake, they don't mind a little colorful language, but I warned him about dropping the f-bombs here. Between those and that New York accent of his, he was doomed from the start."

"Candace, this is America. We have the right to—"

"Don't give me that 'comedic license' bullshit, Drew. You know better." Strong words coming from Candace. "You men are supposed to learn at an early age that you don't point that thing into the wind when you have to pee."

It's hard to argue when you don't have a leg to stand on.

THE DRESSING ROOMS in this club are much nicer and cleaner than the ones we usually get. The lights weren't so bad tonight either, so I'm not all sweaty and sticky. All things considered, I'm feeling pretty good even though I know my first test is tonight.

They went light on the stage makeup, so all I

need to do is wipe my face with a baby wipe. I've just finished cleaning my eyes when I hear a knock on the dressing room door and someone calling my name.

"Yeah, come on in."

Ralph, the stagehand, has a lascivious grin stretching from ear to ear. "There's a lady out there asking for you. Looks like it's your lucky night, she's a real looker."

"Oh really? Where do I find her?" It's been two years since my divorce, and between preparations for this contest and the tour itself, I've had zero time for a social life. Two years is a long dry spell for me. Even the possibility of it breaking starts the stirring of anticipation south of my belt buckle. But my hopes are dashed quickly when I remember that Duffy has my little test scheduled for tonight.

"I'll show you where she's sitting." Ralph is shaking his head in unfeigned admiration. "Not that you'll have any trouble spotting her. Dark red hair, legs for days, jade green eyes and a dress to match them." It's hard to believe that his grin could get wider, but it does. "Too pretty for a place like this."

I don't believe in coincidence, but as I follow Ralph out to the VIP section in front of the stage, there's a shred of hope fluttering in my chest. When I reach the table, she stands up, and my pulse rate skyrockets. Ralph was right. She is gorgeous. My brain tells me there's no way this woman can be part of my test. She's too damned conspicuous, riveting the eyes of every male in the building. Hell, the women are staring at her too.

Her eyes jump out at me first. Ralph's description was woefully inadequate. I swear, there should be a picture of them in the dictionary beside the words "bedroom eyes." They are jade green all right, but huge and glistening with thin streaks of tawny gold radiating from her pupils like the spokes of a wagon wheel. They're set wide over high chiseled cheekbones that frame an elegant nose. Her dress really does complement her eyes, but it also hugs her body in all the right places. Ralph was dead on about one thing: the woman has legs for days.

"Can I call you Drew?"

"You can call me anything you want." Lame, but I can't think of anything else to say.

Her hand is outstretched, and I take it. It's so warm and soft that it takes me a few seconds to notice the slip of paper between our palms. Her lips, the same dark red shade as her hair, never move, even though I can hear the words she's saying quite distinctly.

"Close your hand when you let go of mine."

I jerk my hand back from her touch, looking down to make sure I've wrapped my fingers around the paper.

"Don't look at it," she chides behind a coquettish smile. She sits and casually indicates for me to do the same.

I don't know what I expected, but I can say with absolute certainty it wasn't her. I know I have a stupid grin on my face, but I don't care.

She leans forward across the table, the hand I haven't yet touched snaking out towards me. I reach for it without thinking.

Again, her lips don't move, and her smile never wavers. "Your *empty* hand, dumbass."

It's awkward, but I manage to switch hands without ever revealing the slip of paper in my right fist. Now her lips move when she speaks to me in a low husky voice. I lean until our foreheads nearly touch. Anybody watching us (that is, everybody in the club) will disbelievingly assume I'm getting lucky. I wish.

"Clumsy," she derides, but croons it. The table is small, and I can feel her knee blatantly pressing against mine. I can't help myself. My eyes drop down, and sure enough, a slit in the side of her dress exposes a great expanse of smooth creamy thigh. Despite the state of my nerves, excited chills race crazily along my spine.

"I have no idea what to say now." My lips barely move.

The delicate tip of her pink tongue slips from behind her soft lips, deliberately tracing the upper one. Then she gives me a smile that is absolutely wicked. There is no way I can stand up right now.

"Don't say anything at all, Drew. We're going to have a drink, and then I'll make a show of handing you my hotel room key. As far as anybody here is concerned, you're about to get lucky." She speaks in a low murmur, carrying me away.

"Am I?" I don't need her to tell me I'm stupid. I already know, and she's not going to answer. I signal a waiter and order a double scotch for myself. She asks for a tonic with a slice of lemon. I need the scotch. We don't talk any more, just gaze into each other's eyes. I can't help myself; I'm lost in hers.

I am completely unaware of how much time has passed when she reaches into her small handbag, drawing out a card key and placing it in my hand. She stands and leans across the table, bringing those lush lips millimeters from my ear and incidentally giving me a tantalizing glimpse down the low neckline of her dress. Everybody in the club must be watching us.

"Give me a couple of minutes, and then follow. My room is down the hall from yours." Her hand slithers to my right thigh. I might explode. That wicked tongue of hers flicks out and gently licks my left earlobe. Correction: I might now *be* exploding. I'm going to have to give her more than a couple minutes before I stand up.

"YOU NEED A LOT MORE PRACTICE."

"You threw me for a loop!"

Her mouth twists in a moue of mild disgust. "You were supposed to be caught off guard. It was a test, dumbass."

"Would you mind calling me Drew? Dumbass feels a little too familiar for a first date."

"It's not a date, dumbass. I'm here to conduct an evaluation, and you," she jabs a finger into my chest, continuing her mixed signals, "are treading on thin ice."

To my surprise, she turns around and reaches for the zipper on the back of her dress. Without thinking I reach out to help, but she already has it down, offering a VIP view of the bare skin of her back. But before the dropped fabric lands at her ankles, she has pulled a thigh-length sweatshirt over her head. After stepping out of the circle of her dress, she manages to pull on a pair of skinny jeans without revealing so much as a knee. One slender, elegant hand reaches up, grasps that gorgeous auburn hair, and tugs it from her head, exposing a shocking pink pixie cut.

"Better!" Without bothering to ask, she walks over to the minibar and pulls out two miniatures bourbon bottles and a bag of chips. "God, I haven't eaten all day."

I mentally calculate how much that's going to cost her and make a wry face.

"I can afford the back charges, Drew."

"You know about those?" But of course she does.

"That reminds me. Hand me my purse," she demands more than asks, ignoring my question. It's a habit I'm noticing about her—one I know I'll come to hate. I pass her the little checkbook-sized bag and watch her lift a blank envelope from it.

"Here." She hands it to me and then twists the top off the first of the miniatures.

I stare into my hands, unsure what to do with the surprisingly hefty envelope.

"Go ahead, Drew. Open it." She seems to lose interest in me as she tilts the tiny scotch bottle to her lips.

I slit the top of the envelope with my thumbnail and shake out its contents. My breath catches in my throat. A stack of crisp one hundred-dollar notes falls into my hand. In a trance, I count them one by one. Two grand. Four weeks' pay.

"What is this for?"

"You were told you'd be paid for each of the tests, Drew. You've been paid."

"But this is *two grand*. This is serious money."

"And this is serious business. The agency is damned selective about who they recruit. You should consider yourself lucky."

I didn't get that sense when Duffy handed me this opportunity. Wouldn't he have done the same for Matt if he had complained about buying sodas? "Who else *is* in on this?" The doubts creep in. Life experience has taught me that if something seems too good to be true, it probably is.

"That's a no-no Drew. We don't ask questions if we want to keep getting paid. You've been told that once, you won't be warned again."

I bristle at her thinly veiled threat. The sweet temptress from the club has gone. The pink hair had me fooled at first, but now I recognize the woman facing me for what she is: a ravening beast.

"While we're reviewing the rules, Drew, I need to give you a few more. If you break any of them while I'm training you, the money stops. Cold. You'll be back to making it work on five hundred a week. You know what that means?" She's not about to wait for a response. "You lose that cramped apartment and the crap in it. That crummy car of yours will be repossessed."

I don't know how she knows so many details about me. Maybe she's just assuming my apartment and car suck. Either way, my gut tells me I'm not going to like these rules. Still, I can't look petrified. I bite back the naked fear and try a little bravado.

"What are the other rules, Red?" I'll be damned if I'm going to call her Pink.

She doesn't seem to hear any confidence in my voice. "From here on out, no more cell phones, no more credit cards. When you absolutely must make a call, do it on a landline. When you buy something the tour doesn't cover, use cash. What we have in mind for you is not illegal, but there is serious money involved after your training. More serious than that," she adds, gesturing to the bills still in my hand. "People connected to our clientele spend vast amounts of money to circumvent our efforts. That includes hiring the best minds in digital forensics and other technologies that I don't have time to explain. The point, and the only detail that matters to you, is no cell phones or credit cards. We need you completely off the grid."

I'm standing with my mouth open, speechless. I'm in over my head. The two grand suddenly weighs a ton in my hand, but I can't seem to let it go. I need time to think.

"That's pretty hard talk at somebody you want playing spy games for you."

"Drew," her face is deadly serious now, and I can't detect a hint of insincerity in it, "this isn't a game. The agency and its clients, as well as the people opposed to their efforts, don't suffer bullshit. The amount of money involved on all sides surpasses this country's gross national product. People have no idea that a remarkably small sum of cash could buy their death."

I can't help my voice from raising. Is she saying what I think she's saying? "Nobody said anything to me about getting *killed*."

"Settle down, Drew." Her voice softens. Suddenly she isn't as terrifying as she was a moment ago. Her eyes twinkle with a subtle hint of her earlier sensuality. "There's no danger to you if you follow the rules and do as I tell you. The rules simply ensure your movements outside the tour can't be tracked. That's all. There's more to learn—a lot more—but that's why I'm here. To teach you."

Her hand is on my arm, which tingles from the distinctly sexual contact. Alarm bells stop clanging in my head, but I'm still not completely convinced.

"You can opt out of this at any time during your training. But consider sticking with it for a bit. The money is good, and it gets better after each successfully completed task."

Her blatant sexuality is disconcerting, but I know I need time to think, money or no.

"Do I have to answer right this minute?"

"I said you can *opt out* at any time before your training is completed." She stands on her tiptoes and brushes her lips against my cheek. "You need to work on your listening skills, Drew, but we can talk more tomorrow." Every time she says my name that way it sends my senses reeling. Worse yet, I can feel my skepticism beginning to melt.

I'M LYING in my lonely hotel bed with my hands behind my head, my eyes staring blankly at the ceiling. Unease rolls in my stomach, and I'm doing my utmost to dampen it. I'm a grown man trying to earn a living by making people laugh. It's something I'm good at, but I'm facing the cold hard fact that other people out there do it better. Polishing my routines is draining. Analyzing my peers' performances is more demanding than I ever dreamed it would be. And what's the return? A woefully inadequate five hundred bucks a week, and the slim possibility of similar opportunities once the tour is over. This tour could boost my career, but it's not a guarantee. Frankly, it's not the kind of tour that leads to more tours. I can visualize emerging higher on the food chain, but I can't even guess at how long it will take to get there.

But Red and the agency? Maybe that's an

opportunity. Two grand? Just for meeting a gorgeous but certifiable wacko after a show and letting her leave a Post-it in my palm?

I bolt upright. I never looked at the note. I just balled it in my fist and tried to look casual as I thrust it into my pants pocket.

My pants are draped over a chair beside the bed, and I stumble over my shoes in my haste to get to them. The note is a wadded-up little ball at the very bottom of the righthand pocket. My heart flutters as I uncrumple it, then deflates. All it says is "good job.'" Two grand? Every logical cell in my brain screams that something is very wrong about this. Twenty brand new hundred-dollar bills lie in my hotel safe. They are screaming a lot louder than my brain cells right now.

CHAPTER FOUR

ALBUQUERQUE, NEW MEXICO

I HURRY to finish the scotch the flight attendant brought me, because the pilot just announced we're making our final descent into Albuquerque. I hadn't even wanted the scotch when I paid the passenger beside me to order it, feigning a lost credit card and handing him some cash. But I was feeling celebratory.

I'm glad to have had it once I've disembarked. Everything at this airport is so bright and colorful, and I'm jubilant as I walk across the concourse. My misgivings are gone, at least for the moment. Until the tour is over, I get to do what I love, and the money has given me the confidence to believe that I can still achieve my goals. What Duffy wants me to do is a minor distraction. I can deal with that.

Feeling this good puts a bounce in my step that has been missing for a long time now, and even dour old Bob has remarked on it, even though we rarely talk to each other. My good mood diminishes only slightly when I spot Duffy waiting at the concourse entrance as all of us tour members approach.

"How was your trip?"

I wonder how he got here before we did. I sort of expected him to travel with us since he is responsible for all travel arrangements, but so far, he hasn't even ridden on the bus with us for the short trips.

Duffy gives Candace a perfunctory hug, and he makes sure to shake everyone else's hand. He makes me a little nervous, though, when he wraps an arm around my shoulder and accompanies me to the bus, deliberately slowing our pace to let the others walk out of earshot.

"I'm told you passed your first test with flying colors, Drew. Congratulations."

"Nothing to it." I'm showing a little swagger even though the hackles on the back of my neck start to rise. It's not like Duffy to sound even remotely sincere in his dealings with me, so I'm waiting for the other shoe to drop.

"Good, good." He squeezes my shoulder firmly and confidently, once again uncomfortably reminding me of a used car salesman. "I've got another test set up for you, Drew," he murmurs. "We're going to try another pass tonight, but it's not going to be as simple as your first test. We need to see how adaptable you are— whether you can think on your feet." He winks at me and leaves me frozen, flabbergasted at the door to the bus. As he walks away, without bothering to look over his shoulder, he calls out, "Got a conference call. See all of you at the club before the show!"

I still have doubts about this whole deal, but as far as I can tell, I'm not in danger, and I'm not breaking the law. A small voice in my head insists this is all too easy —that it can't possibly be on the level if it's worth two grand. Even so, I bought an overpriced drink on an airplane, my apartment back home is paid up through the end of the month, and thanks to the extra cash I shoved into the overnighted envelope, I managed to convince the sleazy landlord to send checks on my behalf for the utilities. The one cost I didn't bother with was refilling my prepaid phone, being that Red forbade me to use that, too. I'm reminded it's still weighing down my pocket, and spotting a trash container a few yards away, I take a moment to dump the flip phone inside it before climbing aboard the big motor coach. The bus driver gives me a dirty look for taking my time, but I return a friendly grin and make my way to the vacant seat beside Candace.

I'M GEARED toward a blue-collar audience, so the artsy-fartsy crowd in Albuquerque makes me a little nervous. Albuquerque is famous for its art community, so there's bound to be a lot of highbrow. The best thing I have going for me is that they're mostly older. I shake off my nervousness when the emcee introduces me, and I stride onto stage like I own the joint. The first few lines don't go over as well, as I expected. Screw it. I launch into my alternate monologue, charging ahead like I planned it this way.

"We played fun games when we traveled. For one game you had to roll down your window. Yes, to the younger people in here, you used to have to *roll* down your window. By hand. And by the way, our windows went *all the way down*. None of this halfway bullshit. Back in my day, we knew how far you could hang out before you fell out of the car. Back in my day, we had depth perception. I didn't need the government telling me how far my step-kids could stick their bodies out before they fell. And a lot of times that back window would even come off the track and disappear into the door, remember? No dad fixed that. You just had a trashed back door for the rest of the trip.

"But you would take your seatbelt—which nobody made you wear when I was growing up, because I grew up with the generation of parents who could give a shit about child safety. And you knew your parents didn't worry about your safety because nobody had a problem with you sitting on the front seat armrest as you went to grandma and grandpa's house. You'd just be riding along in their grey Caprice Classic, thinking, 'Being able to see kicks ass, man! Look it! I'm higher than dad's compass. Going to grandma's and gonna eat that weird ass grandma ribbon candy.' I've never seen that shit in stores my entire life, but every grandma has it on a green dish on her coffee table. When you go to grab a piece, it's stuck so hard the whole coffee table lifts up.

Because two generations of your family licked that candy. All of your cousins would watch like it was some initiation.

"'Can I eat it?'

"'I don't know, dude. Give it a try. Welcome to the club.'

"But nobody cared you were on the front seat armrest, no seatbelt, hanging on your dad as he drove.

"Meanwhile, all the windows are rolled up, the ashtray is loaded in front of you, and everybody's smoking.

"'I love Pall Mall. No filters.'

"'So do I. Cigarettes are never going to be bad for you.'

"'I know, right?'

"I remember talking to the seatbelt and pretending it was a CB the entire trip. Just to age myself, that was my whole trip from Detroit to Florida, I would be, 'Breaker. Breaker 1-9. Big Bear, this is Rubber Duck. Come on back.'

"For you people in your twenties, CBs were like Facebook in the seventies."

I DON'T FEEL like my performance was flat tonight, but I don't feel that special connection with the audience either. It has just been one of those nights. It doesn't matter, though, because I know that I'm about to get another windfall if I'm up to the challenge—or up to

Duffy's standards, anyway. I don't even bother going back to my dressing room. I just accept a couple of cleansing wipes from the makeup artist to clean my face off and ease my way out into the audience during the intermission.

Everybody is polite and the handshakes are friendly enough. Of course, at least one celebrity groupie is always in the crowd, and tonight is no exception. This time it's a pretty damned good-looking and obviously wealthy matron at least ten years older than I am displaying an astonishing amount of cleavage. Her husband, however, only has eyes for the skimpily-dressed blonde twenty-something sitting across from them. From the calculating look on the blonde's face, she's assessing the older man and considering an upgrade from the anemic accountant-type who brought her to the show. I have to confess: under other circumstances, I might have been tempted by the jilted matron. The look in her eyes leaves no doubt that she is eager to add one more name to her list of conquests.

My mind, however, is on someone else entirely. I scan the crowd for dark red hair. Albuquerque is known for its eclectic upper crust, but I don't believe Red will show up without her wig. The pink would call attention to herself, and she will be trying to blend in. I'm learning; at least, I think I am.

I make my way around the room, a smile on my face and some amusing one-liners on my lips. It's all very ordinary, except for the fact that my eyes constantly move, looking for her. A sinking feeling grows in the pit of my stomach—a feeling that I've missed her somehow. Shaking my head a little as if that will clear it, I almost do miss her. It's hard to keep recognition from showing on my face, not to mention my surprise. She's blonde this time, and she's wearing a demure, floral-print young mom dress and comfortable flats. Nothing shows on her face as she takes my hand and shakes it. She's good.

"I really enjoyed your show. Will you be coming back to Albuquerque again soon?" Red's voice, with a marked southwestern twang, is soft and unassuming, just audible beneath the noise of the crowd.

"I don't think so. At least, not until the tour is over."

"That's a shame. I would have liked to bring my husband and kids to see you perform. It's seldom we get comics here who don't lace their performance with vulgarities just to get a laugh. You're very refreshing."

Our conversation is over just like that, and she's gone. It's over so quickly that I nearly drop the matchbook she's left in my hand. I somehow manage to awkwardly stuff it in my pants pocket before I shake the next hand thrust at me.

NOT DARING to take out the matchbook in front of anybody, I hurry to my dressing room so I can look at it closely. A matchbook. It's comfortably sentimental, reminding me of a time when I'd try dozens of phone number combinations to reach a girl whose number I'd rubbed partly off the coated paper. They used to give these things away everywhere as cheap and effective advertising. That was in the days before lighting up a cigarette became a hanging offense. Being a smoker these days places you somewhere between lepers and child molesters in the social order. Unless your flavor of tobacco dependency is cigars, like Ron White. Now there's a guy. A natural born comedian, funny as hell, drinking booze and smoking cigars on stage in front of God and everybody. The man has balls of solid brass.

The matchbook is kind of nondescript, has the name of some no-tell motel on the front in block letters over a cartoon of a man and woman kissing. Subtle. Inside the cover there is a single handprinted word: *suitcase*.

The hotel is half a mile away, and it's all I can do to keep from running back to it. I don't even bother changing out of my stage clothes. As nonchalantly as I can manage, I take a leisurely stroll back to the hotel, pretending to enjoy the night sights of downtown Albuquerque while my mind races at a hundred miles an hour. Honestly, I don't know which thought has me more excited: the prospect of seeing Red again or finding out what's inside my locked suitcase.

Outside the door to my hotel room, my hand is trembling, making it difficult to fit the key card into the thin little slot that will unlock the door, but I manage. I gulp so loud that I nervously glance up and down the hallway to see if anyone heard me. I'm not sure whether I'm feeling fear or anticipation. Probably a little of both.

Holding my breath, I enter the room and scan it quickly. It's empty; doesn't look a bit different than it did when I left it such a short time ago. If there's anything in that suitcase, though, somebody had to have come in.

My suitcase is lying on the bed, right where I left it. The tiny little key to the suitcase is on my key ring and my hand is still shaking so much that it takes two or three tries to fit it into the little holes on the clasps. I need to get a better suitcase—clearly one with a sturdier lock. But I dismiss that thought as soon as it crosses my mind. I keep my cash in my carry-on, not my luggage. I don't trust baggage handlers. Even if I could bring myself to, I have no desire to be detained by TSA. They don't just look for weapons and potentially dangerous fluids. Those jerks are curious about everything. Once they put all five of us into a waiting room and interrogated us just because someone heard Matt make a stupid joke about another passenger looking like a homegrown terrorist. No sense of humor.

When I open the suitcase, there is another sealed white envelope lying on top of my carefully folded clothes. I don't bother trying to slit the length of the envelope this time. I tear the end off and shake it once. More crisp one hundred-dollar bills. I slowly count out twenty-five of them before letting out a low whistle. Twenty-five hundred bucks for a handshake and a short, unremarkable conversation? The money doesn't feel so heavy in my hand this time.

I could get used to this.

I CAN'T SLEEP KNOWING there's over three-and-a-half grand in my hotel safe, let alone replaying a slow-motion mental video of Red unzipping that crimson dress and letting it drop to the floor. Maybe I should've taken up that horny matron's not-so-subtle advances. With a great deal of effort, I manage to shift my mind to a slightly less pressing problem: what to do with the cash. Part of the solution occurs to me right off the bat. I'm going shopping, and this time I won't be looking at the sale racks in some discount store. I have three more days here in Albuquerque. Time enough to visit a real tailor. I can't spend it all—there will be more bills to pay at the end of the month, and I'm not sure how long it will be before this money dream peters out—but for however long it lasts, I need something do with all the cash. Sooner or later somebody is going to want to know where I got it all.

THIS HOTEL IS SWEET. There's a nice workout area I'm not tempted in the least to use and a heated indoor pool. We don't have to check out until tomorrow morning, and I'm riding a high from my new cash flow and the possibility of seeing Red again soon for more training. I'm not that big on swimming, but the hotel waitresses serve drinks poolside in abbreviated uniforms, and I am *always* big on that. It never occurred to me to bring swim trunks on tour, but there's a gift shop in the lobby.

After hurriedly passing by the speedos (Who wears those anyway?), I find a pair of jazzy cobalt blue trunks. The legs have palm tree silhouettes, which don't thrill me, but at least they're not embarrassing. I'm feeling flush, so I don't even blink when the brilliantly smiling cashier tells me I owe sixty bucks and some change. She's hot, and I want to impress her, so I flash a small roll of hundreds and try to look cool as I peel one of the bills free and hand it to her. I know it's a bush league stunt as soon as I do it, and I can feel the crimson blush flooding my face. I should know better. I'm not usually such a pathetic excuse for an adult. I take the bag she hands me without making eye contact and slink out the door. I hate the kind of guy who does that crap, and I cannot believe I stooped so low.

I change into the trunks in my room, still pissed at myself but determined to wear the trunks that cost me sixty bucks and my dignity. I refuse to let a foul mood overshadow my excitement at finally being able to enjoy the finer things in life without guilt or worrying about money.

I slip on my hoodie and stalk down the hallway to the elevator, which takes forever to get to my floor and open, putting more unwanted time between me, that pool, the waitresses, and a strong drink.

When I get to the pool, I realize that I forgot to bring a towel with me, and I struggle for a minute to regain my cool. But the beautiful aqua water looks blissfully soothing, and except for the waitress and bartender at the far end of the pool, I have the place all to myself.

Desperate not to repeat my mistake, I approach the patio bar with the least amount of swagger possible and order a Glenfiddich, neat. It seems odd to drink a nice scotch from a plastic cup, but I'm thrilled at the prospect of sipping a drink while floating carefree in the pool.

I strip off my hoodie and toss it onto one of the deck chairs, kick off my shoes, set my scotch on the ledge, and plunge headfirst into the warm water.

Leaning back in the water, arms spread wide, I let the warmth soothe my jangling nerves. The irritability begins to leave my body. I decide to swim a few laps to work off what's left of my pique. I realize I'm only annoyed with myself for trying to be someone I'm not. I let the money go to my head for a minute, flashing that wad in there, and I have to remember not to forget how hard everything seemed a day ago. Hell, things still seem hard. Money isn't going to change how well I perform. But at least it will help decrease my stress. Starting with this drink in this pool.

As I'm coming back to the end of the pool to sip my scotch, I spot a couple standing by the chair where I left my hoodie. The lady is not bad looking, but the guy is a behemoth, wearing, of all things, one of those speedos from the gift shop. He's a big slob of a man with Dunlap's Disease (his belly done lapped over his speedo), so when he turns around to face the pool, he doesn't appear to be wearing anything at all. The smart thing for me to do would be to give them a smile and wave and swim away. I try.

The lady, dressed in a demure one-piece the same color as the pool, gives me a timid smile in return and then glances at the behemoth nervously. Speedo gives her an angry look and me a baleful glare. All I can do is shrug and get back to my laps. It doesn't help. Tension has returned to my shoulders and neck, and I know I'm wasting my time. This is turning out to be just one more bad idea.

I make another lap, at speed, trying to exorcise my inner demons I guess, but when I return to the end of the pool and climb out of the water, Behemoth has his big ass planted on top of my hoodie—and he's grinning wickedly me. I'm ready to snap.

"You're sitting on my hoodie."

He gives me a sneer in response and stands up belligerently. "And what are you gonna do about it?"

His eyes are slits, his face is beet red, and I know two things right off the bat. One, he is *spoiling* for a fight, and two, he is *way* bigger than I am. I'm no chicken, but I'm not stupid either. This situation calls for tact and a considerable amount of cool.

"No problem, man. I'll move it. I was going back to my room anyway." I pick up my drink in my left hand and try to step past him to reach my chair.

"Dwayne . . ." the demure woman warns tentatively. "He didn't mean anything by it. It was just a friendly wave. Don't you remember? He's the funny guy from the show last night."

If anything, her timid defense of me pisses Behemoth off even more, and he slams into my shoulder with his beefy forearm, knocking me away from the hoodie.

"I didn't think he was funny," he snarls.

The waitress and bartender are watching this tableau with open mouths, and worse, the cashier from the gift shop has come outside and is staring at me too. I snap. I turn around and bring my right fist up from somewhere around my right ankle, intending to take Behemoth by surprise and knock him flat on his ass. Wrong move. I'm a comedian, not a boxer, and Behemoth reads my intentions from the word go.

I have just enough time to take a deep breath before he tackles me, drink and all, into the water. I'm no candy-ass, but I'm not much of a brawler either. Did you ever try to fight in the water when your feet don't touch bottom? It's like fighting in Jell-O; everything is in slow motion. I land a couple of blows, but there's no steam behind them, and I realize I've got no idea how to get out of this.

I can see his big fist coming, but I can't get out of its way. He connects with my jaw, and I literally see stars.

The next thing I know, I'm lying on the pool deck. The bartender is bent over me, while the cashier and waitress stare down at me with big, sympathetic eyes.

"Man," the bartender says, "are you alright? That dude was huge! Why'd you swing on him?"

My jaw hurts like a bitch, but I stare up at the guy in disbelief. I didn't start the fight.

I don't bother answering and head to my hoodie, but when I lift it off the chair, a torrent of water runs off it. Apparently, Behemoth wasn't satisfied with kicking my ass.

I can see my audience try to dart their eyes away. They probably watched as that asshole dried his fat rolls on my clothes. There is nothing I can do to redeem myself in front of these kids. Nothing at all.

I storm back to the elevator and the sanctuary of my room and the refrigerator of miniatures. I'm gonna fire up YouTube, knock back a *full* drink, and see if I can find a video that tells a guy how to fight in water. If I'm going to be a spook, I might have to know how.

CHAPTER FIVE

CRAFT TALENT AGENCY HEADQUARTERS

Wilshire Blvd., Los Angeles, California

TODD RAINEY SAT in a deep soft leather armchair so low to the floor that he couldn't see the top of the massive mahogany desk before him. The vast corner office he had been summoned to was near the top floor of Wilshire Boulevard's new modern building. Lush, thick pile carpet stretched from wall to wall, and the ornate furnishings clearly hadn't been purchased from some supply catalog. Original paintings, not prints or cheap knockoffs, decorated the walls not occupied by floor-to-ceiling plate glass windows. Objets d'art dotted the room's various tables and display pedestals.

As if his surroundings weren't intimidating enough, the other leather armchair was occupied by a ravishing redhead stylishly dressed in a denim jacket, skinny jeans, and wicked boots with stiletto heels—an outfit undoubtedly purchased in one of Rodeo Drive's exclusive boutiques. Even in Los Angeles, a generations-old mecca for gorgeous women and men seeking fame and fortune in the motion picture industry, this woman would stand out like a rose among the thorns. She didn't seem to care Todd was staring; she pretty much ignored him.

Todd stood when a man wearing an impeccably tailored pinstripe suit entered the office and sat down in the chair behind the desk. The woman did not.

"Todd Rainey," Todd said as he offered his hand, but the man didn't take it, nor did he speak. Todd sat down. He still didn't know this guy's name.

The man clasped his hands across his waist, then nodded at the redhead. Finally, after a long moment, he turned his gaze back to Todd.

"I know who you are. I sent for you." He turned his face back to the redhead. "How's Drew doing? Has his performance been satisfactory?"

"Pretty good actually. I threw him a curveball by altering my appearance. He handled himself pretty well."

The man cocked his head to one side, obviously thinking. "Think he's ready for the next step?"

"Possibly, but I'd feel better after a few more trial runs. Making them progressively tougher would allow for a more accurate evaluation."

Feeling left out, and in his opinion, entirely too important to be ignored, Todd couldn't keep his mouth shut for another second. After all, he was Drew's manager. "Just who is Drew going to be working for? I'm not complaining, you understand, but we're talking a lot of money for some simple tests."

The man did not turn his face away from the redhead, but his ice blue eyes swiveled back to Todd and fixed him with a stony stare. "Twenty percent of Drew's take just for sitting on your ass and doing nothing seems more than generous to me. If that's not enough to quell your curiosity and keep your mouth shut, then perhaps Drew might be persuaded to retain a different manager who will rob him for less."

Todd's mouth audibly snapped shut. He had survived years of Hollywood fuckery, and he hadn't done so without learning to recognize a threat when he heard one. He knew now that he was only present at this meeting as a sop to his ego. Participation had never been part of the agenda.

The man leaned forward, resting his elbows on the desk and steepling his forefingers against his lower lip as he mulled over the woman's statement. There was no sound in the room for a full five minutes. Finally, he wove his fingers together and placed his palms on the desk. He didn't even bother to look at Todd.

"Mr. Rainey, I don't think we have any further need for you . . . today, that is. I think I would be remiss in my responsibilities if I did not take this opportunity to remind you that nondisclosure is a critical element of CTA's agreement with you. This is a very sensitive assignment, and any breach of contract would carry . . . consequences."

Todd didn't need further clarification. Drew was on his own.

"SO, YOU THINK DREW HAS POTENTIAL?"

The woman leaned back in her chair, more relaxed now that Todd Rainey had cleared the room. She wasn't comfortable discussing details in front of someone who wasn't need-to-know. Shared details led to shared secrets—secrets that she didn't want shared. The fact that she was ten years older than she looked was a closely guarded one. The fact that she had spent those ten years conducting clandestine services for the United States government was another. The man sitting across from her was one of a handful of living people who knew about her skill set, and even he didn't know the full extent of her experience. Already, Drew calling her Red hit too close to truth. Few people inside the American intelligence community were aware that the Soviet Union maintained a swallow school outside Moscow during the Cold War. The cadre of the school had been subsumed by the Russian mafia after the fall of the Soviet Union. The school has since been operated on a for-profit basis, and she had voluntarily completed the courses there after leaving the employ of the U.S. government.

"Yes, provided you give me the time to train him."

"And that would entail what, exactly?"

"Situational analyses first, and then we can get into specifics."

The man gave a knowing look. "You're thinking Monito?"

He was referring to Isla Monito, something she was considering, though the uninhabited island, accessible only by helicopter, housed one of their most private training camps.

"Authorize several more trial runs, and I'll let you know."

The man reached down to the lower righthand drawer of his desk and withdrew an unopened bottle of Blanton's and two squat tumblers. He gingerly opened the bottle and poured two fingers of the bourbon into each glass. He held one up to the light, swirling it around as he did so. Apparently satisfied with what he saw, he handed the tumbler to the woman.

Patience is an essential skill for clandestine operative, the absence of which tends to shorten one's life. The woman kept her mouth shut, enjoying the bourbon's subtle citrus and spice notes—the warming vanilla and oak. At length, the man set his drained tumbler on the surface of his desk.

"Your standard fees satisfactory?" he asked.

"For the trial runs, yes. For Monito, if we decide to go that route, I think I'm due a ten percent increase over my standard fees. A girl's got to keep ahead of inflation, you know."

The man hesitated for a half-beat before saying, "Consider it done."

No unnecessary small talk followed. The meeting was over, and the woman got up and left the office. The man at the desk stared at her as she walked out, and when the door shut behind her, he reached for the telephone.

~

NORMALLY SHE LIKED to drive fast, but she hadn't chosen the rental car for pleasure. She had taken a nondescript sedan from the rental agency at LAX and driven straight to Wilshire Boulevard. With the meeting concluded, she had no further reason to stay in LA. Drew was still in Albuquerque, but his tour itinerary would take him to Vail, Colorado, in two days. There would be no show in Colorado, however. CTA was comping the tour cast and crew for four days' downtime before their next show in LA. It was an unusual perk for the group, but the agency had an ulterior motive.

Near Vail, the woman owned an isolated cabin, a former Federal Witness Protection Program safe house that she had bought for a song at a government auction once it had outlived its usefulness. It was a great place to relax and collect her thoughts. It would also give her the privacy she needed to conduct some rather rigorous physical evaluations of Drew.

She thought about Drew as she drove. He wasn't movie star handsome, but there was something about his face and his manner that attracted her to him. She was going to have to set and observe strict boundaries for herself during the rest of his training to ensure her bias didn't affect her judgment. She had not lied, however; he did have potential. And after his training was over, she could reassess the topic of boundaries. The next six days would not be easy ones—for her or for him.

CHAPTER SIX

EAGLE COUNTY REGIONAL AIRPORT

Vail, Colorado

THE AIRPORT here is a lot nicer, and bigger, than I expected. I guess nicer is not the word I should've used. Vail, after all, is a resort town, and there are no cheap seats here. The concourse area has lofty exposed-beam ceilings, and everything is as sparkling clean and fresh as the air outside. I've got a good bit of cash in my pocket, and I'm looking forward to four days of what we used to call R & R back in my army days. I know this is a ski resort, but I don't plan on doing any. I don't mind the cold, though, and I'm willing to bet I could rent a snowmobile instead. From what I could see of the scenery as we flew in, this place is absolutely breathtaking. If Lady Luck is with me, I might even find a snow bunny to wine and dine—and possibly relieve myself of my involuntary celibacy.

I guess I'm lucky already; our next show won't be until after we reach LA. I won't be looking for Red for the next four days. I know she's off-limits, but she fires up my libido in a way no woman has since I was in high school. Maybe I can start looking for some company now. Looking around the concourse, I already see some interesting possibilities. I'm looking forward to spending a couple of days relaxing instead of honing my skills as a comedian. Everybody has to take a break once in a while.

My good mood lasts until I reach the front entrance, where I see Duffy. The used-car salesman grin on his face tells me R & R isn't on the itinerary for me. On the other hand, if he's planned another little test for me, I might get to see Red. That prospect is not altogether unsettling.

As usual, he hugs Candace first before shaking hands with the rest of us. Again, as usual, he shakes my hand last. "There's a shuttle bus waiting for all of you out front. I need to talk with Drew here for a minute—a little personal business to take care of—so I'll have him brought on out to the resort later." He's got his hand on my shoulder again, holding me back as the others trundle out to the shuttle bus.

"Thought this was supposed to be R & R?" I phrase it as a question, my right eyebrow raised sardonically. His response is not at all what I'm expecting.

"Not for you, Drew. In fact, the next four days may be the opposite of relaxing. On the bright side, this will be your biggest paycheck yet. I don't think she's got anything particularly rough set up for you," he chuckles, "but with her, you can never tell."

My eyebrow drops back to its normal position and a tentative smile begins to form. "Red's here?"

Duffy gives me a funny look. "Excuse me?"

"Red. My trainer?"

"I didn't know that's what you called her."

"She's never told me her actual name, so . . ."

"Well if she hasn't told you her name yet, I'm sure as hell not going to. I barely know her, but I would not want to piss her off. I've heard stories about her." He shakes his head from side to side. "In any case, you're not going to the hotel. You're spending the next four days with her. I already told the skycap to take your luggage out to her car. She will be taking you on to where you're going to be staying. Now," he says, clearly preparing to jet on me again, "I've got to catch a flight to LA in just a few minutes."

"Wait a minute. I think I deserve more explanation than this. Where is she taking me? What am I going to be doing?"

Duffy's expression is one of exasperation. "Do you like the money, Drew?"

I shrug my shoulders. "That's kind of a stupid question."

"Then don't ask *me* stupid questions."

To say that I don't care much for his attitude would be an understatement, but I did just hear him say that this would be my biggest paycheck yet. More money, I get to see Red, and he doesn't think she has anything particularly rough in store for me. Frankly, my curiosity —and my celibate body—is aroused.

"Then let me ask you another kind of question, Duffy." I lower my voice. "I'm not comfortable running around with all this cash on me. I'm afraid TSA will scan it and give me a hard time. Is there another way we can handle my . . . payments?"

"Let me think about it, Drew. I'll take it to the higher-ups and see what they can come up with. That's the best answer I can give you right now. In the meantime, I've got to catch my flight, and you need to get outside now. She's been waiting."

There's no time for any more questions. Duffy is already speed walking toward the ticket counter.

THE AIR IS crisp and biting cold outside, but the wind is calm. The airport maintenance personnel are on the ball here. The snow has been blown off all the paved surfaces, leaving the sidewalks and streets clear. I do a double take when I see Red, donned in boots and jeans, leaning against a clone of OJ's white 1992 Ford Bronco. Her thumbs are tucked into her pockets, the heel of one dogger-heeled cowboy boot propped against one of the outsized tires. She sports her pixie hair, but it's now the same shade of dark red as the wig she wore when I first met her.

"Fancy meeting you here, Tex!"

I'm rewarded with a balled-up fist, middle digit extending upward. It makes me laugh.

"Funny. Get in, dumbass. They already brought out your bags." She called me dumbass again, but as we get in the Bronco, there's a crooked smile on her lips. I'm beginning to think it's a term of endearment.

I find the way she is dressed intriguing, and the view of her backside as she walks away is enticing. I'm still not sure what's in store for me, but if I had known I was going to spend the next four days with Red, I would've been happy to do it without being paid for it.

In the Bronco, I'm grateful for the heater. It suddenly occurs to me that I didn't pack real winter clothing. I needed the space in my suitcase, so I'd planned to pick up a parka and whatever else I might need at the resort gift shop during this leg of the tour.

The monster tires on the Bronco make a loud yet pleasant humming rumble inside the toasty warm passenger compartment, and the ride is surprisingly smooth. Red handles the big SUV like a pro. I see a sign indicating that the resort I was supposed to be staying at is four miles ahead. Before us, the road has been cleared of snow as far as I can see, but the smooth ride abruptly ends when Red turns onto a side road that hasn't seen the blade of a snowplow yet. She seems to be following two narrow strips of packed down snow, but the farther we drive, the more trouble I have making them out. Red, however, doesn't slow down one bit.

"How can you tell where the road is?"

"Who do you think made the tracks going out?"

I can't think of a response. This ride is starting to get scary. We are climbing the side of a mountain, and just off to the right of the outermost track, the land seems to drop off into nothingness. I try to look nonchalant as I grab the handgrip above the window, but I can feel my butt cheeks clenching together and my feet pressing hard against the floorboard. I'm a city boy, and this shit scares the hell out of me. I give Red a sideways glance, and I see that delicate pink tip of her tongue poking out between her teeth, her brow furrowed in concentration. Even so, her hands grip the steering wheel firmly, not tightly, and her shoulders are relaxed. She appears totally confident. Wish I were. I squeeze my eyes shut so that I won't have to see the drop-off to my right, and a mercifully short time later, the Bronco comes to a stop.

"You can open your eyes now, hotshot. We're here."

We've stopped behind a low and long log cabin with a pitched metal roof. Off to the right is a path leading downhill toward a large, weathered wooden barn. A cluster of smaller outbuildings, constructed of the same weathered clapboard as the barn, stand beside it. It takes me just a few seconds to figure out that the barn and outbuildings are far older than the log house.

"What is this place?"

"It's mine. It used to be a government-owned safe house, but I got a good price on it when they auctioned it off as excess property. The original cabin on this property burned down, and the place was abandoned.

The IRS took it for back taxes, and it was appropriated by the clandestine services because of its remote location. They rebuilt the main house and upgraded the outbuildings."

She has never been this talkative before, and I can sense that she is distracted, thinking about something else as she rattles on about the place. I'm curious as to what's on her mind, but I don't think now is the right time to press her.

I hop out of the Bronco and grab my new suit bag and matching suitcase from the back. Red is already at the back door, but not waiting for me. She's not even looking back to see if I'm coming.

The inside of the cabin is a real surprise. I'm not sure what I expected but it certainly wasn't this. Most of the cabin is taken up by a huge great room. A stone wall inset with a massive fireplace dominates one end of the room. The mantle is a split log coated with a thick layer of varnish. In the wall opposite from me, a vast picture window looks out over a deck, which juts out above a deep valley. The wide hallway to my right presumably leads to the bedrooms and bathroom. The furnishings—the stocky armchairs and thick wooden coffee table, the cage lamps and buffalo plaid blankets—have a distinctly masculine character.

Red turns to face me, her arms folded across her chest. Her face is expressionless. I can't read it.

"We have four days here together. I understand Duffy told you that payment for this session will be larger than usual. That's true, but I don't think he told you that payment for this one is conditional."

"No, he didn't." It's taking a minute for that to register. "What conditions?"

"You have to follow my instructions to the letter, and you must satisfactorily complete every task that I assign you. If you don't, I'll take you down to the resort and leave you with the others. You won't be paid for this session at all if you don't perform. And—"

"And that will be the end of . . . whatever this is we've been doing?"

"Yes." I hear no inflection in her voice. I detect no emotion in her face. Those green eyes bore into me, and corny as it sounds, peer at my naked soul. This is giving me goosebumps.

Though I already know what my response will be, I hesitate. I'm going to do whatever she says, but I'm not willing to let her believe she has me completely under her thumb. "Okay, done," I agree after a long while. I think I see a flicker of relief in her eyes—brief but there.

"Good. Take your bags down the hall to the last room on the right. You can put them in the closet. I don't think there's anything in them that you're going to need, unless I missed something." She turns to look through the big picture window, dismissing me.

The hallway is a little longer than I expected with several closed doors on either side. The last bedroom on the right is open, and I walk right on inside.

If anything, this room is more masculine than the great room. The king bed's headboard and footboard appear to be made from limbs sawed off the tree yesterday. The mattress is covered by a thick wool Navajo blanket that matches the drapes covering the window. On either side of the bed sit a heavy dresser and mirror, and an armoire made of dark wood. A thick board with four-inch pegs is nailed to the wall beside the door, presumably to hang clothes on.

I open the closet to put my suitcase and new suit bag inside, and I find it already contains a couple pairs of jeans, a flannel shirt, one of those commando sweaters I see on TV all the time, and a black knit watch cap. There's a pair of brand-new L.L. Bean hiking boots on the floor. I know without looking that everything is in my size. Red is too damned thorough to make that kind of mistake.

In the dresser are enough underwear and socks for my stay, along with a belt and a pair of gloves. She's thought of everything except maybe a snowmobile suit . . . but I have no idea whether there's a snowmobile here or not. I wouldn't put it past her.

I DON'T WAIT for her to tell me to change. I hang up the ones I'm wearing and slip into the ones hanging in the closet. It takes a second for me to decide whether to go with the flannel shirt or the commando sweater, but the sweater is just so damn slick, I have to put it on. I don't notice her leaning against the doorframe until I sit down to lace up the new boots.

"How long you been standing there?"

"Long enough to see that you need gym time. Your thighs and calves especially could use a little work." A trace of amusement alights in her eyes.

"Yeah, well, I don't think I'm going to be running any marathons anytime soon." I know right off I've said something wrong. But so what if I'm a little peeved? I mean, I know I'm no Arnold Schwarzenegger, but I think I'm in pretty good shape for a guy my age.

"Listen, Drew. You can't take anything for granted in this business. If you do everything right, you should never have to face any kind of physical confrontation at all. The thing is, you could show me someone who has never done anything wrong, and I could show you someone who's never done anything at all. Everybody screws up sometimes, even the best of us. The work you're going to do is not intrinsically dangerous, but the sums of money that ride on the outcome are so vast as to be unimaginable. I'm not sure just how much you have seen, but I've been places in this world where people kill each other just the promise of ten U.S. dollars."

The alarm on my face is real. I got into this mess because I needed the cash and because Duffy swore to me that I couldn't get into any trouble for doing it. He didn't say anything about getting killed. Then again, he chose his words carefully when recruiting me. Just because I'm not doing anything illegal doesn't mean someone won't want to kill me.

"Don't get your panties in a wad, Drew. Nobody's

going to try to kill you, but you can't take anything at all for granted. You know as well as I do that you can get killed by a lunatic just by walking out the back door of a club. Anyone with any sense has to realize that they need the ability to defend themselves. What's the harm in learning how to take care of yourself? In being in decent enough shape to fight back?"

I'm somewhat mollified, especially considering the Great Albuquerque Pool Debacle, but I'm not convinced I wasn't duped into something dangerous. "Be real with me, Red. What kind of danger are we talking here?"

Red stands up straight, her back rigid, her arms across her chest again. The drill sergeant has returned.

"You're an adult, Drew. Live with the consequences you didn't think of. I know you got into this for the money without thinking too hard about the implications. I also know that CTA can make things happen for your career that you could never buy with money. Did you really believe that reality show contest —or any of them for that matter—was won based on skill and talent? Do you think CTA invested all this time and money into you and your manager—into *me*— just because you needed more cash flow? Just because you can stand up in front of a group of people and make them laugh?"

"My manager?" It makes sense Red's getting paid for working with me, but it never occurred to me that Todd would be in the loop. Did he know what he was getting me into when he convinced me (not that he had to try very hard) to sign up for this contest?

"You have a contract with him, right? That means he gets twenty percent whatever you make as a performer. And what you're doing for us is a performance, Drew."

"I, uh, I guess I never thought this all the way through . . ."

"Well, you should have." She shakes her head angrily, and despite the emotional conflict I'm feeling inside, I can't help thinking that she looks especially hot when she's pissed. "I'm going to take a shower. Then I'm making us a pot of coffee, and we're going to sit down so you can tell me if you're in or out."

I RARELY DOUBT my own abilities. I'm realistic in that I constantly strive to make myself more proficient, to polish my act, but deep down, I have never doubted that I have what it takes to be a successful comedian. I'm a little shaken that all it took to make me question myself is a pint-sized redheaded dynamo of a woman who I barely even know.

I can believe that Todd never said a word about the true reason for the contest, but it bothers me that I probably didn't make the top five based on my comedic ability. Probably I was picked because CTA knew they could buy me. It bothers me even more that they were right.

I CAN SMELL the coffee as soon as I reach the great room. Red is sitting at the dining table wearing, as far as I can tell, nothing but a white terry cloth robe. Her bare feet don't even reach the floor, and she has a thick white mug of strong black coffee in her hand. A carafe steams on the table, with another mug, empty, beside it.

She wastes no time on preliminaries. "Have you decided?"

I ignore her blunt approach. I'm not going to let her think she bullied me into this decision, even though she's had an undue influence. "You said CTA can do things for my career?"

I detect not a smidgen of duplicity in her green eyes. "They can make you a star, Drew."

"And this side money? I keep getting it as well?"

She nods. "Untraceable and nontaxable. Once I assure them that you're fully on board, CTA will set up an anonymous numbered account for you in the Cayman Islands, and all funds you earn will be deposited there."

"What happens if I'm out?"

"Then I drop you off at the resort unpaid, and none of this ever happened."

I already know my answer. I'm not happy with where I'm at as a professional stand-up comedian, and I'm not happy being a half–assed spook either.

I'm going to learn whatever Red can teach me, and then I'm going to milk CTA for whatever I can get out of them.

I am tired of the grind.

~

AS I WASH up the breakfast dishes, I'm exhausted. Red looks like she spent the last three days at a high-end spa. Over those days, she has constantly teased me, flirting with me one minute, going Ice Princess the next. I've even caught several glimpses of her in various stages of undress, but she has managed to end those before anything serious could come of them.

That first day she insisted on going over the different methods of executing a brush pass, something seemingly simple but comprising an endless variety of variations. Even so, it was kind of boring. The next two days were more interesting. I immersed myself in the mysteries of the one-time pad cipher. Mathematically unbreakable, it relies on a pre-shared key, making it mostly impractical nowadays except for protecting something never to be shared. Surprisingly, it's easier to use than it might sound.

I also endured hours-long lectures about spotting a tail while riding in the OJ-mobile so I could practice the techniques.

I've no idea what's in store today—even less so when Red walks into the kitchen wearing a catsuit. I'm not sure what it's for exactly, but it fits her like a second skin, sending my libido into orbit. A soapy plate slips from my hands, clanking loudly in the oversized metal sink.

"Meet me in the barn, Drew. Ten minutes."

I have no idea what she's got in mind, but the way she's dressed, I don't really care.

This is the first time I've even been inside the barn. If this place even has lights inside, she hasn't turned them on. I guess I expected to smell hay or horse manure or something like that, but instead the strong aroma of sawdust overwhelms me. A few short steps into the dimly lit barn tells me why. The floor is coated with the stuff, and I'm soon ankle deep in it. For some reason, it feels creepy to me.

I can't see clearly in the gloom, but I can sense that the space in front of me is cavernous.

"Red?"

No answer.

I try to shut out everything except my hearing. I have a hunch about the game she has planned, and for the first time since this little training trip started, I feel the playing field level. If I'm right, this is a game I've played before.

WHEN I FIRST GRADUATED COLLEGE, and paying gigs were few and far between, it occurred to me that joining the National Guard would provide me with some much-needed extra funds to help me bridge the gap between paychecks. I tried the Air National Guard recruiter first, but I didn't get any play from him. The Marine Corps sounded a little too gung ho for me, plus, as you now know, I hate deep water. I ended up talking to the guy from the Army National Guard, and he told me the only spot open was in an infantry unit. I was ready to give up until he convinced me that it would be easy to transfer to a technical unit if I was already in the Guard. I was pretty gullible in those days. Yes, more gullible than now. Needless to say, it was revealed, by a crusty and extremely sarcastic drill sergeant, that I had been misinformed.

To my everlasting surprise, I didn't hate it. In fact, I excelled at it, particularly in the hand-to-hand combat training. As a matter of fact, I was so good at it that when I returned to my parent unit after advanced individual training, I was chosen to assist in training my peers. The senior NCO that I was assigned to assist was a martial arts instructor in civilian life, and he took an interest in me, getting me involved in the discipline more or less recreationally.

I FALL into a horse stance without consciously thinking about it. I'm blinking my eyes rapidly, an infantry technique to improve my night vision. It works. I can see the vague outlines of support beams—the tufts of chewed up wood on the floor. I catch the merest hint of someone breathing softly, and I strain to pinpoint a location. It's above and behind me.

A loft.

Still in horse stance, I rotate one hundred and eighty

degrees on the ball of my right foot and plant my left foot solidly in the sawdust. Not fast enough. She drops on me, planting both feet on my chest and knocking me flat on my back.

Still working to catch the breath she knocked out of me, I try to hook my right leg around her neck, but she ducks, bringing her face in close to mine. She's strong, and she's tenacious as hell.

Her forearm presses into my throat, and spots shimmer before my eyes—a sure sign I'm about to pass out. In my desperation, I manage to free one hand, get it behind her head, and pull down, smacking her face—and her lips—into mine.

I'm not sure at what point everything changes. In one moment, her teeth are mashing into mine as if she's trying to grind me into submission. In the next, her lips are going soft and pliant, melding with mine. I am acutely aware of her breasts pressing against my chest, and hyper aware that she is straddling the physiological manifestation of my gender—an excruciatingly pleasant turn of events. She lifts her head up, those fascinating green eyes boring into mine from a distance of no more than three inches. I don't make another move.

"Never let up just because your opponent is a woman. It takes only thirteen pounds of pressure on the human jaw to render a man unconscious." Then she proves it to me.

∾

I COME to staring up at the barn rafters. The lights have blinked on, but Red is nowhere in sight. Groggy, I stagger through the barn door and make my way into the snow. The Bronco is gone from its parking spot behind the cabin. I have a sinking feeling that my four days with Red are over.

And that it hasn't ended well for me.

CHAPTER SEVEN

LOS ANGELES, CALIFORNIA (DOWNTOWN)

I'M UNEASY. Red left an envelope containing six thousand dollars in my suit bag, so apparently, I somehow passed that stage of my training to her satisfaction. I haven't seen her since our hand-to-hand episode in the barn though.

Duffy isn't waiting at LAX, which makes me a little apprehensive because LA is his home base. Where the hell is he?

He doesn't meet us at the hotel either, and that's a first. I'm thinking maybe I jumped the gun by assuming Red gave me a pass after our session at the cabin. The prospect of never seeing her again, as well as CTA choking off my wellspring of ready cash, is more than a little disheartening.

On the brighter side, the downtown club venue is new and ultramodern. Plush theater seats in a multi-tiered arrangement encircle the floor by the stage. VIP ticket holders sit at small round tables covered with fine damask tablecloths. An aura to the room tells me I'm going to have a good night. The stage is elevated, and for once, I have a well-lit vantage point that doesn't blind me.

~

"GROWING UP, I swore I was going to be kidnapped. My teachers did a great job of making me afraid of strangers. To this day, when I'm out in public, I'm still vigilant for potential kidnappers. It's something I try to teach my stepdaughter. I'm like, 'You're just oblivious. You have no idea how many people are standing around you. Take your face out of your phone every once in a while and put eyeballs on people.'

"To this day, if I see a rundown van, my first thought is, 'I am *not* helping that guy find a puppy! Stranger danger! Chester the Molester!'

"I recently had carpeting installed. The guy is like, 'Why don't you come out to the van, and I'll give you the receipt.'

"Fuck you, dude! I'm not coming near that van! I lean in the passenger seat to grab that receipt, next thing you know, I'm putting lotion in a basket. It's not happening.

"We played outside a lot, and I had to deal with the threat of the van guy, because I had a dad who worked nights. Clap if you had a parent who worked nights." I get mild applause. "See how hesitant they are?" I say to the rest of the audience. "Because they had parents who worked nights and they're not *allowed* to make noise."

"We're the quietest people because nothing got you into more trouble than waking that parent up during the day. I still have vivid images of my dad bounding down the hall after we'd woken him up. He worked the UPS third shift. He'd be stripped down to his tighty-whities, but still wearing his brown UPS socks, and that would always put the fear of God in us.

"Even now when I see a UPS guy, my first thought is 'Everyone just be quiet for a second.'"

MY INITIAL ASSESSMENT was right on the money. Tonight's crowd loves me. I had one of those magic moments with the audience. A pretty woman at one of the front tables found my crack about LA traffic so hilarious that she snorted with her mouth full of champagne, spraying it all over the tablecloth and her companion. I was rendered speechless, cracking up for a full twenty seconds—a long time when you're performing in front of a live audience, but they were laughing with me. Classic comedy that only works in person.

My euphoria is short lived. I'm pretty sure I have scrutinized every face in the audience, even the ones in the theater seating, and I haven't caught a glimpse of Red yet. I know I shouldn't worry. But it is the first time I haven't been given some kind of heads-up from

Duffy upon my arrival. I haven't felt this insecure since right after I finished college.

The ushers are letting some of the audience members from the theater seats onto the VIP floor, so I have to turn my attention to them. The third person to shake my hand, a rugged man with a military haircut and a seamed, weathered face, looks vaguely familiar. His left arm is wrapped around the shoulders of a very attractive blue-eyed blonde who looks several years younger than he is.

"You probably don't remember me, Drew, but I remember you all right. Stecker. Bill Stecker." A huge grin splits his face. "You might remember me better as 'Drill Sergeant.'"

Recognition dawns on me, and I cover our handshake with my left hand as well. "You're looking great, Sarge!"

"You're looking pretty good yourself, Drew. Looks like you've got yourself a pretty sweet gig." He turns and introduces the blonde to me as his wife. I don't have time for an old home week; the ushers are politely urging us to move along because the last set is due to start in a few minutes. I'm actually tickled to see Stecker again, and I'd like to talk with him for a few minutes after the show. I keep an eye on him and his wife as I finish schmoozing with the fans, taking note of where they sit down so that I can locate them again.

The overhead lights blink twice, indicating that the next set will start in exactly five minutes. Something, I don't know what, registers in my brain, making me glance back at Stecker. He's sitting next to a dowdy elderly woman who has both her hands resting on the cane planted firmly between her knees. She has wispy gray hair and loose, wrinkly skin, but the eyes peering out of that ancient face are anything but old. They're jade green, streaked with gold. It's Red. I know she's seen me, but right now she is studiously avoiding eye contact.

The lights dim, and a spotlight shines on the emcee as he takes center stage. "And now, ladies and gentlemen, fresh from four days' rest at Eagle Point Resort in Vail, Colorado, courtesy of our sponsors, Mr. Bob Thomas!"

Bob is not the most popular of the finalists, and a few people get up and leave during the act. As soon as it's over, my eyes flick to where Stecker is sitting. Sure enough, Red has already gotten up. Leaning on her cane, she is shuffling past everyone's knees toward the end of the second row to get to the aisle to the lobby.

I shake hands with the last few fans remaining on the VIP floor and make my way toward the aisle as quickly as I can without calling attention to myself. Red is moving faster than an old lady with a cane should be able to, and by the time I reach the lobby, she is nowhere to be seen.

"So, what have you been doing with yourself, Drew?" Stecker and his wife have followed me into the lobby.

"Same as before I joined the Guard, Sergeant Stecker. I worked the club and campus gigs wherever I could find one until I built up my rep enough that I could afford a manager. When my enlistment was up, he put me on a local club circuit, and I've been working more or less steady ever since." While I'm talking to him, my eyes constantly scan the lobby for any sign of Red. Sergeant Stecker doesn't seem to notice.

"No need to call me sergeant anymore, Drew. It's Bill. I'm retired now. Twenty years. It just doesn't seem possible."

I open my mouth to frame some kind of innocuous remark, but he's already talking again.

"I was just saying to Lila that we should ask you to our home while you're in town. I could lay on a case of beer, throw a rack of ribs on the smoker, and we could rehash old times." I spot Red coming out of the ladies' room. She has ditched the old lady get-up for a pair of khaki slacks and a green pullover shirt that she must've been wearing under the muumuu. She's moving in my general direction, but not very fast. I recognize her gait. I saw it many times before, when we practiced the brush pass.

"I appreciate the invite, though I may have to catch you next time around. Let me use the restroom quick, and then I'll grab your number. Would you excuse me, Lila?" I don't wait for an answer. I walk towards the men's room on a path that will intersect with Red's. In the intervening distance, I mentally review everything she taught me about the brush pass, and I remember it all except for one major detail. I've practiced passing items to Red a hundred times or more. I don't remember practicing the reverse. And she's going to be passing something to me.

In trying to look like a guy hurrying to the men's room, I'm already moving too fast for the pass. As I approach Red, who is still painstakingly avoiding direct eye contact with me, I panic and try to change my own gait. I muff the brush pass and watch a yellow Post-it flutter to the lobby carpet. I am mortified. My face turns beet red.

"Hey, Drew!" Stecker shouts out. "You dropped something!" My eyes are squeezed shut, and I'm wishing the floor would open up and swallow me whole. Bill Stecker's big hand drops onto my shoulder, and he's holding the Post-it in his free hand.

All I can think to say is, "Uhhh, thanks . . ." before snatching the small paper square from his hand and scurrying toward the men's room like a rat deserting a sinking ship. My uneasiness from earlier in the evening has turned into full-blown despair. I'm screwed.

I make my way to the last stall and latch the door behind me. I'm sweating like a pig, and my hands shake with rage and frustration. I have screwed up by the numbers, and I'm convinced that Duffy is going to drop me like a hot rock. I'll be lucky if he doesn't bounce me right off the tour!

It takes me several minutes to calm myself. When my hands are no longer shaking, I reach into my pocket and pull out the crumpled yellow slip of paper. It's covered with tiny printed letters and numbers in blocks of five. It's an OTP cipher . . . but I don't have the key, damn it! I roll my eyes. I'm not quite sure how my day could get any worse, but I have a sneaking suspicion that the worst is yet to come.

I need a drink.

I STUPIDLY ENTER my hotel room before looking for the paper I placed between the door and the jamb. It's now lying on the carpet, but I can't tell if it fell just now, or if it's been lying there because someone else has been here. Get a grip on yourself, Drew.

The room looks pretty much the same as I left it, but I have learned too much in the last few weeks. I go to the closet and check my suit bag. The near invisible piece of cellophane tape is still in place over the zipper track. The tape on my suitcase is there as well, but on closer inspection, I notice it has been peeled off and then carefully replaced, but not carefully enough. I haven't been given a real-world task yet; I'm still in the training phase, so I know that Red has to have been the one who tampered with my suitcase. There's no reason for anyone else to have come in here. Nobody except CTA knows I'm carrying around a stack of cash in my suitcase—or even that I have a stack of cash.

As soon as I open the lid of my suitcase, I see the encryption key lying on top of my commando sweater. To anyone unversed in the principles of one-time pads, it would look like a block of random numbers and letters. To me, it looks like hope.

Decrypting the message is tedious for me. I understand the procedure, but I'm slow at it, especially because Red's tiny block printing is hard to read without a magnifying glass. After laboring for a couple of hours, I find where I made a transcription error. The corrections take mere minutes, and the end result comes as something of a shocker.

Completed Phase I training. Envelope front desk. Open in private.

The desk clerk is a sleepy kid in his twenties, and I have to show my ID to get the envelope from him. It's thick, but not as thick as the one Red left me at the cabin. There's a smudge on one corner of the pristine envelope this time, but it's late, and I'm tired, so I won't even bother to look at it closely until I get it upstairs.

I've been through the wringer, and I haven't even changed out of the clothes I wore for the show. Despite my curiosity, I force myself to destress before diving into the envelope.

After stuffing the envelope into my pillowcase, I double check the locks on the door and then turn on the shower as hot as it will go.

While I'm toweling off, I decide that a celebratory nightcap is in order. Chivas Regal is my elixir of choice tonight, and I pour the contents of the miniature into a plastic water tumbler from the bathroom.

I carry my drink to the bed and stretch out, taking a small sip. An image of the envelope materializes in my head, particularly the smudge in the top right corner.

None of the envelopes I've received so far have had a mark on them. I know it has to mean something. Flipping on the lamp switch next to my bed, I reach inside the pillowcase and retrieve the envelope.

Under the light from the lamp, I examine the smudge closely. There's something there . . . but I can't quite make it out. Setting the tumbler of scotch on the night table, I sit up and move to the desk where the light is brighter. I rub my finger over the smudge and feel the indentations where something had been written. The smudge is actually an erasure. But how am I supposed to read the indentation?

An episode of a forensic science show pops into my head, and I grab a pencil from the desk drawer. First, I erase the smudging completely. Then I look around for something sharp. I wish I carried a pocketknife (something, I realize, I need to remedy), but I have to settle on my cheap disposable razor. Carefully, I make a fine powder by shaving the pencil graphite, allowing the powder to fall over the indented area of the envelope. I don't have an ostrich feather brush like the scientist on TV had, but I fluff out a cotton ball from my shaving kit and lightly brush the graphite around before blowing the remaining powder off.

The number three shows up startlingly clear. What the hell?

That's a mystery, but I'm too tired to think about it tonight. There's another three grand inside the envelope. I add it to my stack, then wrap it with a rubber band and stuff it into my suitcase. I really need to do something about that.

THE NEXT MORNING, I'm staring at the envelope, trying to change my mind. The only conclusion I can draw is that I'm not the only one being trained right now. And the only reason for an envelope to be numbered is if it's been in a stack with other envelopes. I'm no detective, but I can put two and two together—even if it takes me a while.

I go down to the hotel desk and see the same kid as last night. A lucky break for me. When I approach the desk, he smiles, recognizing me, but I put on a confused face.

"Are you sure you gave me the right envelope last night?"

His face immediately blanches. "Oh no. I knew I would mess that up. But yours was the only one left."

My stomach jumps. Of course I was right. But now I'm feeling dumb again, because I don't think this kid knows what to do next. He's turning red, fumbling over the phone to see if he's by some miracle place another envelope elsewhere on the desk.

"It's not a trouble. I know the person who might have gotten mine. I'm not sure what room they're in, though."

"Okay, which one of them was it?"

I take a second. At least two of the other tour

members are in on this if I'm number three. I have to assume Candace would be one of them. She's smarter than me, and I have to hope Red isn't training the other men and putting the moves on them, too. The thought makes me sick. And jealous.

"It would have been Candace Murray."

"Okay. Yeah, she's in 305."

"Great. Thanks," I say, turning toward the elevators.

"Sir? I'm not technically supposed to give you this information, but seeing as how I've messed up, I wanted to help you. Just, you didn't get it from me, okay?"

"Get what?" I wink.

"SORRY. You can service the room later."

"Candace? It's Drew."

"Drew?" She opens the door and her red hair is mostly hidden by the towel wrapped around it.

Now that I'm at her door with no obvious reason for being here, I'm not sure how to start a conversation. What could I possibly need from Candace that I couldn't wait to ask until the show tonight?

"Uh, can I come in?" I stall. Stupid! If Red were watching me, she'd be calling me an asshole. I really am one if I think I can get information just by knocking on a door. If Candance is being trained the same as me, I am sure she is going to be careful not to say anything. More careful than me anyway.

"Sure, Drew. I was just about to head down to breakfast, though. Do you want to join me down there?"

"It'll only be a minute," I say. I don't want to get wrapped up in a meal with her if I'm ultimately not supposed to know she's part of the training, too. On the other hand, how would I suspect another tour member is being trained. We all know each other. It wouldn't be out of the question to have breakfast with her. Except, I haven't done that on any of the other runs, so if Red happens to be here in cognito, I don't want her to get suspicious. Damn.

"Okay. Come on in," she says. "Is everything all right?" she asks once she's closed the door behind us.

"I'm short on cash," I stammer.

"Oh. I have to say, I wasn't expecting that."

Had she been expecting me to ask about Red? Does she already know I'm being trained?

"I'm sorry, this wasn't appropriate of me. Please forget I asked."

"No, Drew. It's okay. I can lend you something if you need it. I get it. We're only managing to scrape by on this tour, even with help. God knows I'm lucky I kept my day job as long as I could. I was able to save up some so that I wouldn't have to worry about scrounging. How much do you need?" She walks over to her handbag and pulls out her wallet.

Now I feel bad. If she really isn't training, I'm outright stealing from her with how much money I'm making.

"Uhh. Two hundred should do it, I think. But really, anything you could help me with."

She opens her wallet and frowns, then replaces it and digs further in her purse. I can't see what she's doing, but when she turns around to face me again, she has two bills in her hand.

Two crisp hundreds.

"I know this goes without saying, but I expect to be paid back by the end of the tour. I know it's hard, but if you don't manage the money they're allowing you, you're going to come off this tour broke."

If she's giving me this advice, and her money, she must not suspect what I now know. She's definitely in training, but she has no clue anyone else is doing it, too. Or at the least, she has no clue I'm doing it.

"Thanks, Candace. Really. And I know this goes without saying, too, but I'd appreciate it if you didn't mention this to any other of the tour members."

"Of course, Drew. Be careful, okay?"

Be careful? So then, does she know?

I'm supremely confused.

ONCE I'VE HAD coffee and some breakfast, I head to the hotel lobby, planning to take a walk to clear my head. I know it was stupid of me to fish for information from Candace. I'm starting to think she purposefully gave me that crisp bill to send me a message. In fact, I'm sure of it. Candace is the sharpest one of us here.

She's probably following whatever training she's receiving by the book. Her career as a comedian matters too much to her to risk it. Giving me the hundred that so clearly came from a pile in a white envelope? That was her telling me that she knows what I am doing, and that I need to keep pretending that I am just a confused trainee.

Message received.

I head outside and wince instantly. I should have known that a leisurely stroll through downtown LA wouldn't be as relaxing as I was picturing it. I decide what I really need is quiet, and that means somewhere inside and away from the traffic. It's early, but late enough that the Museum of Art will be opening soon. It only takes a second for me to hail a cab and start heading west.

Unfortunately, once we've made our way onto Wilshire, traffic is an utter horror show. I try to see what cross street we've made it to, and as luck would have it, we're only a few blocks away. I pay the cabbie and let him know I'm happy where I've gotten to. He only seems slightly miffed, probably because he can turn around in the next alley and avoid the rest of this hell himself.

I head west on Wilshire, now more hopeful at the prospect of a few quiet hours to myself, when I catch sight of someone I recognize walking on the opposite side of the street.

Jason. At first, I'm ready to wave and call his name, but then I stop myself.

I don't know if my training's kicking in, or if I'm now just paranoid that everyone's deeper in this than I thought. But now I'm wondering, why is Duffy here when he's based in Detroit? He has nothing to do with the tour.

I do my best to remember all of Red's tips on how to tail someone as I try to make myself inconspicuous. I shift further into the crowd and make sure not to enter his peripheral vision. My heart hammers in my chest, even though I'm the one who's supposed to be here, in LA, because somehow, I know I'm not supposed to be *here*, following him.

It feels like a lifetime, but it's only blocks when he finally stops at a modern-looking building, most of the front made of glass, and enters.

I don't know what he's doing there, or who he's meeting, but I am certain of one thing.

CTA is bigger than it seems.

Much bigger.

CHAPTER EIGHT

SAN DIEGO, CALIFORNIA

"GOOD MORNING, Mr. Roberts. This is the 8 a.m. wake-up call you requested for Room 1222."

"Thank you. I appreciate it."

I should've canceled the wake-up call; I've been up for half an hour. I've been preoccupied. I don't know what I've gotten myself into. I know a lot more people are involved, and CTA doesn't want them to know the extent of this industry. There's also question that I'm reeling over Red's mixed signals, especially because I haven't spoken with her since the barn. To make matters worse, I'm still worried about Duffy. Where the hell is he? Why hasn't he contacted me? There's no doubt about it; I'm feeling antsy as hell.

Worst of all, I still feel as though my ego's been cheated because my talent didn't get me on this tour. But I'm still looking for fame and fortune, and I still believe I can make a career of stand-up. I just have to accept that it's going to take more than talent and effort. I need the muscle that CTA can give me, and that means I need to be a better spook too.

I know in my heart that Red has cut me some slack in my evaluations, no question about it. I can only speculate as to why she's done what she's done. I need to get my head out of the clouds and stop fantasizing about a relationship with her. I need to get serious about this spook business. Not only is it money in the bank. It's the key to my future.

I'M the last one to climb onto our charter bus to San Diego, and I make my way down the aisle with no more than a curt nod to acknowledge Candace's friendly greeting. Everybody seems to be studying their notes for tonight's show, none of them looking as shaken up as me, and I realize that nailing my act has not been my priority lately.

I'm not ready to go over my notes yet, so I lean back against the seat and clasp my hands behind my head. Everything Red taught me at the cabin is still fresh in my mind, so reviewing it is fast and easy. I'm tempted to linger over the memory of our wrestling match in the sawdust—the feel of her lithe body pressed against mine, her knees straddling my hips, and the taste of her lips. It's a struggle to suppress that memory, but it's a struggle I have to win. I am determined to concentrate on the skills she worked so hard to teach me instead of my boyish fantasies.

As the driver eases the bus into morning traffic, I drop my hands to my sides and close my eyes. I know I should be going over my bit for tonight, but it's hard for me to focus. Even before the bus shifts out of first gear, I feel it lurch to a stop, and I hear the hiss of the doors slamming open.

Curious, I lean over in the seat and peer down the aisle. The bus driver says something in greeting, but I can't make out who it is. It has to be Duffy. Everybody else is accounted for . . . unless one of the stage crew members missed their bus last night.

It's not Duffy. Oddly enough, it's some kid with a battered old army boonie hat pulled down low on his forehead, wearing a denim jacket, jeans, sneakers, and a canvas backpack. Head down, the kid makes his way down the aisle, the bus door slams shut, and the bus starts moving into traffic again. I figure I was right about a stagehand. My curiosity no longer piqued, I lean my head back against the seat and close my eyes again. As luck would have it, the kid plops down in the seat next to me . . . and now I'm annoyed.

My eyes pop open, and I look directly into a pair of eyes that are such a weird shade of blue, I know he's wearing contacts. I'm about to say something rude when I recognize the kid's face. My jaw drops open in surprise, but before I can get a word out, Red is reading me the Riot Act in a voice so low I'm sure no one else on the bus can hear it. She hurls a torrent of vitriol at me, the likes of which I haven't heard since basic training. The tirade goes on for several minutes before I can get a word in edgewise.

"Why are you giving me hell? I know I flubbed the pass, but I recovered the paper and decrypted the message, didn't I? Even your note said I completed the first phase of training successfully."

Ripping the boonie hat off her head and slamming it down on the seat between us, Red shakes her hair out. The pixie cut is still there, but it's a little shorter and dyed black. It's amazing how different her face looks with the black hair framing it and the weird blue of the contacts shining out from new bangs. Even the disguise can't hide the fact that she's beautiful, but she's still talking to me through gritted teeth.

"Honestly, Drew. You've got to get serious about this business. Believe me when I say, you can't afford to make even the smallest mistake. Your fieldcraft has got to be letter perfect." A little of the tension goes out of her face, and she leans her head back against the seat. I look around to see if any of the other comedians noticed her outburst, but only Percy looks up to meet my glance, and he just smiles and waves.

Could that mean I'm wrong? She's not yelling at any of them. But maybe she's only here for me? Then again, maybe I'm the only one who messed up.

I settle back into my seat, not daring to look at Red. I'm still confused about that, too. Why did she pass me to the next phase of training if I am such a screwup? It doesn't make sense. And so what if I did foul up. I'm still in training, right?

She doesn't speak again until the driver slows down to negotiate the interchange onto I-5.

"I can't do it, Drew. I won't. This next phase of your training is critical, and you're going to have to get through it on your own." Her voice drops down to a whisper, barely audible over the noise of the bus engine. "When you're through with your training, failure to execute your assignments perfectly can have consequences. Dire consequences, Drew. That's all I can tell you right now, and it's all you need to know. Dire consequences."

The chill in her voice and her choice of words scares the hell out of me. I'm not sure how to respond. It's obvious she is genuinely scared for me, and that in itself makes me pretty damned nervous. Everything I know about Red tells me that she is not the type person who scares easily. She is bold, fearless, supremely self-confident, and as I gleaned from personal experience, physically fierce. I want to know what has her so worried, but I'm afraid to ask. I shut my mouth and lean back in my seat, my mind racing at full speed.

There is no doubt in my mind now that there is more to all this than I've been led to believe. Jason in LA. Others being trained. The money, plus Red's fighting skills and her knowledge of spook fieldcraft. If CTA is willing to pay me this much just for training, Red has to be making bank. Whatever it is they have in store for me, it's not as benign as I've been told. The question in my mind is whether the success and money are worth the unknown risks involved. I'm a little ashamed to admit, even to myself, that I know the answer. A very large part of me is not only willing to accept the risks, it's excited by the prospect. I want this.

I look straight at her. "I won't let you down again, Red."

"I'm not worried about you letting me down, Drew. I'm worried that I've let you get in over your head." She sounds tired. I feel her hand on my cheek and I turn sideways in my seat so I can see her better, my heart racing at her touch and what it might mean about us. "Are you determined to go ahead with this? You're a smart guy, and you must know there's more to all this than I can tell you right now." Her eyes search mine, but her blue contacts are disturbingly distracting, and I'm finding it very hard to concentrate.

"Yeah, I am, Red."

Something, either relief or anxiety, I can't be certain which it might be, sweeps over her face, and she takes her hand off my cheek and leans back in her seat.

"Everyone makes mistakes when they first get started, Drew. What we do takes practice, and not everyone is suited for it. I think you have a natural aptitude, but I don't want to push you into this." She sighs. "I get paid either way, whether you make it or not."

We sit together in strained silence until the tour bus takes the downtown San Diego exit leading to our hotel.

"WAKE UP, DREW."

Red shakes my shoulder. I don't remember falling asleep, and I'm temporarily disoriented. "Come on, we're almost there, and I need you to be awake when I give you your instructions."

I'm awake now.

"I wanted to try another brush pass tonight, but based on that last one, I'm not sure you're ready for it yet. We'll discuss that later and practice it some more. For now, I want you to concentrate on what I taught you about spotting a tail." She picks up her boonie hat from the seat between us and clamps it down over her head, pulling the brim down low over her eyes before standing up abruptly. "This is for you." She presses another plain white envelope into my hand and quickly bends over to sneak a soft kiss on my cheek.

I barely have time to be excited over her kiss. "What's this? I've already been paid." We've been talking in whispers, but I'm hard pressed to keep my voice down.

"That's a bonus for completing Phase I. I wasn't supposed to give it to you until I made sure you were firmly committed." She turns without another word and races down the aisle to tap the bus driver on the shoulder. He nods, pulls to the side of the road, and then she's gone.

Once she is out of sight, I glance down at the envelope in my hand. It's thick, very thick, and a closer look reveals another barely visible impression in one corner. I wonder if it's another number, but I'll have to wait until I get to my room to find out. I make a mental note to borrow a pencil from the concierge when I check in.

At the least, I know I've had advanced practice with reviewing how a tail acts. I just wish I didn't still feel so suspicious when I know in my gut I want to do this.

THERE IS DEFINITELY an imprint in the top right corner of the envelope, but the pencil shavings don't bring it out like last time. I glance down at my watch to see if I have time to locate a novelty shop before the show. Plenty. Even though the suite (I got an upgrade this time, no explanation offered and still no word from Duffy) has Wi-Fi access, I'm not allowed a laptop or a cell phone, so I decide to go down and talk to the concierge.

I'm in luck. The concierge, dapper gentleman in his early 50s, is a showbiz groupie who harbors a secret yen to become an illusionist. He's more than happy to direct me to his favorite novelty shop, just a few blocks down from the hotel. I should have seen it when we came in, but frankly, I wasn't looking for it then.

Within minutes of entering the store, I spy a child's detective kit containing exactly what I need. When I get up to the register to have my purchase rung up, I realize that the only cash on me is in the sealed envelope Red gave me on the bus. The rest of my cash is stashed under the liner of my shaving kit back in the suite. I don't want the cashier to see me open the envelope. Any raised suspicions would be bad for my CTA track record.

"While I'm here, you wouldn't happen to have a good quality money belt, would you?"

"Sure! Hold on just a minute, I'll get one for you." The cashier is all smiles. She's really good looking, but I'm too busy sneaking free a couple hundred-dollar bills to watch her. Besides, she doesn't hold a candle to Red.

True to her word, she's back in a matter of moments with a money belt in each hand. "These two are top-of-the-line, and I think you'd be happy with either one."

"I'm sure I would. Let me take a look." Neither one is cheap, and frankly I can't tell much difference between them. I pick the most expensive one on principle. "This will do fine." She rings me up and asks me if my purchase will be cash or charge, and I hand her one of the hundreds. As she counts out my change, I notice a display on one of the sales tables that gives me an idea that I think is brilliant. Then again, I think most of my ideas are brilliant, so who knows?

I step out of the novelty store with my shopping bag in hand and walk into the bookstore next door. When I come out, I'm carrying a second bag, this one containing a large and very heavy leather-bound edition of the collected works of William Shakespeare. It takes one more stop at a drug store, and I'm fully equipped with a bottle of glue, a steel ruler with cork backing, and an X-Acto knife. It's time to go back to my suite. I have work to do before my first show.

I take no more than a few steps before I get the distinct feeling I'm being watched. I stop in front of the display window of a men's clothing store and pretend to be interested in a suit worn by a mannequin, a garish striped monstrosity in clown colors that only a New York City pimp would be caught dead wearing. I spot the tail as soon as I glance behind me. He'd been sitting in the lobby when I asked the concierge about the novelty store, I'm sure of it. I realize I've screwed up once again after I whip my head back around. I'm not supposed to let him know I saw him, and my sudden movement is a dead giveaway. Damn it!

Forcing myself to move slowly, gawking around at the big city sights like a tourist from the country, I head back for the hotel. I'm kicking myself inside. I briefly consider waylaying the bastard following me and buying his silence. I sure as hell don't want him telling Red about my lousy rookie mistake.

I stop once more, a couple of blocks from the hotel, and this time I use the reflection in the glass storefront to scan the crowd for my tail. He's nowhere in sight. My heart drops in my chest. I start questioning myself. Maybe that guy wasn't the tail. Maybe he just looked like that guy in the lobby. This is San Diego, a town with a million people. I could easily be mistaken.

But then he walks right past where I'm standing, just a little too casually, assiduously ignoring me. That only convinces me more that I wasn't just right about him, but I have screwed up by the numbers. I may have just lost everything.

Second Show

Paranoia. That's the only acceptable explanation. No word from Red or Duffy last night after the show. I spent two hours walking downtown today, keeping an eye out for a tail, but I never spotted one. I even looked for the guy from yesterday, but if he was following me again, he had changed his look completely.

The audience is in a better mood tonight. Matt didn't piss them off, and Bob is following me for the final set. I haven't gotten any news from Red, but no news is good news, and I'm feeling much more confident. I'm ready to go out and wow them.

"I'VE BEEN DOING stand-up for 23 years now, and as a comedian, you wonder when you start to lose the younger crowd. You know? You can't be relevant to everybody. But I always hope that at 20, you'll still pay attention. Even when I say words that aren't in your life right now, like marriage or stepdaughter. I hope you don't tune me out, because here is a lesson. You can learn a lot about life from people who have already lived it.

"The big mistake young people make is thinking they're the first people to ever go through whatever shit they're going through. Walking back to my hotel, I saw some guy leave a club all proud of himself, shouting, 'Man, that was *awesome*. No dude's *ever* run that game on a chick before.'

"Yeah, we all have, dude. Some of us just did it in Members Only jackets.

"So, my young friends, let me just tell you about the shit you can expect. I'm 42, married, I come to you from the future. There will be a time, my young friends, when all those condoms in your pocket magically become Tums. Because one day you'll realize, I've got a better chance of getting a stomachache than getting laid.

"Me, I don't know how to dress my age. I'm too old for Abercrombie but not old enough for Tommy Bahamas. I'm like a tweener, I'm in this weird stage.

"But I look to the guys from the future—the guy who's been through this shit before, right?" I nod knowingly at the crowd. "And I know that eventually, I will get to the Tommy Bahamas age and realize, yes, these shirts are comfortable. Then I will get a little older and realize, yes, visors do keep the sun off. By that time, pants that zip off into shorts will seem like a great idea. Fanny packs? Convenient. Laces? Stupid."

"My grandfather had five of the same pairs of the pants, five of the same shirt, and five of the same jacket. As a kid, I was like, 'Man, it's so *sad*. Every day, my grandpa wears the same clothes.' But now that I'm older, I picture him, and I think, genius! A life uniform? That's the greatest thing I've ever heard of. What am I wearing today? My life uniform. Bam! Next decision."

~

I FEEL PRETTY GOOD. I managed to establish a real connection with the audience tonight, almost as if I were a part of their family. I feel so good I decide to walk the fifteen blocks to the hotel.

After I've changed, I decide to head out. Maybe I can spot that tail tonight after all. I pretty much have to; we'll be on the road to Tucson tomorrow, and I'm assuming that's my deadline.

I'm more careful leaving the lobby tonight. I spend fifteen minutes shooting the breeze with tonight's concierge. He's a younger kid with sandy blonde hair whose every other word is "dude." He's cheerful, though, and he thinks I'm a celebrity, so he is doing everything but wriggling like a puppy because I've stopped to talk to him. While we're gabbing, I let my eyes roam slowly around the lobby. In practice, Red seems capable of committing to memory a considerable number of people, but I don't have that total recall. She told me it's a learned skill, and I'm taking her word for it. It's hard.

Once I've done my best to discern he's not here, I disengage myself from the young concierge and make my way out the front door. It's still early, nine o'clock, and people still move along the sidewalks. It's definitely not as crowded as it was yesterday, which makes it a little easier for me to casually maintain a three-hundred-and-sixty degree surveillance. I make frequent stops, gazing into store windows, reading signs, pretending I'm watching for a cab—every technique Red taught me, I use.

The third time I stop, I spot a man in a camel windbreaker and a Padres hat. He makes the same stupid mistake I made the day before. When he sees my eyes on him, he looks away too quickly. I don't turn my head, but avert my eyes to a shapely young brunette in a revealing dress standing between him and an MTS route sign. I make the best of an opportunity to ogle her while keeping track of him. My nerves settle down. I'm beginning to feel in control of the situation.

My instincts are absolutely on the money. After three more stops I'm convinced. The tail identified, I walk slowly ahead, seeking one of the outs Red taught me to look for. The first available one comes when I approach a major street crossing with a bored looking cop standing beside it. I wait patiently through three cycles of the light change, timing the flashing pedestrian light. Certain that I have the timing down, I wait until the last millisecond before darting into the crosswalk. I don't look back until I cross the street and the building beside me obscures the intersection. At a dead run, I race towards the end of the block, but Lady Luck is with me. A cab stops directly in front of me, and the passenger climbs out. I make it into the backseat and shut the door before the guy even manages to pay the cabbie. I give the cabbie the name of my hotel and relax as he eases out into traffic. The tail knows where my hotel is, but I'll be back there and safely in my room before he can get there. Finally! An assignment I did not find a way to screw up.

RIDING the high from successfully spotting that tail, I open the detective kit and get to work on the latest envelope from Red. Again, the number three shows up after I wipe the excess powder off with the ostrich feather. If I had any doubts left about the other tour members' involvement, they've gone out the window now. The thought is disturbing on several levels. Successive images of Red using the same moves she put on me on all the other performers pop into my head. I don't want to go there.

Forcing my mind away from forbidden territory, I start my book project. The red leather of the Shakespeare volume I purchased is rich and luxurious in my hands, and I feel a twinge of guilt at what I'm about to do. I open to a page about a third of the way through and remove two hundreds from my stash, laying them side by side on the page. Using a pencil, I mark the page outside of the bills with four points, leaving an eighth of an inch extra at each. The steel ruler is useful for connecting the dots I've made. Then, placing the flat edge of the X-Acto Knife against the ruler, I press hard and cut into the underlying pages. I repeat the cuts until I have removed the page centers to a depth of about two inches. I fit two stacks of hundreds inside to see how they fit. Perfect. I sit back, satisfied with my handiwork. All that's left is coating the outside edges of the cut pages with clear glue so that the compartment seals when I close the book. Secret Compartment 101. Who reads Shakespeare anymore?

CHAPTER NINE

TUCSON, ARIZONA

I FULLY EXPECTED to see Red on the tour bus to Tucson, but there is no sign of either her or Duffy. I wonder if that guy in San Diego the first day actually was one of the men assigned to tail me. If he was working for Red, I'm screwed, despite my success the second day. The thought is enough to send me plummeting into a depressing pool of self-doubt and apprehension. Right now, I don't know whether to expect an ass-chewing, a pat on the back, or being dropped from this program outright. It's nerve wracking to say the least, and the bus ride seems to take forever. By the time we get to Tucson and our hotel, I'm in a wretched state.

The fact that I'm in another suite instead of a standard room is a little reassuring, though I'm not certain if the other tour members—or should I say, trainees—have suites, too. I can't help wondering what it means if the others are going through the same training that I am. Does that mean only one of us can succeed? Is this part of the test? Was I *supposed* to figure this out? Frankly, so many of my dreams and ambitions have changed because of the side money that I'm afraid to risk asking any questions. I'm hooked through the bag and I know it.

I'm tired of worrying—about the other tour members, about Duffy and Red, and about my next training task. The bar downstairs is calling my name, so I throw on my hoodie and slip on my shoes. A drink, or maybe two, can't hurt me, and I'm tired of the miniatures in my room. I've got a taste for a decent single malt scotch.

THE BAR IS DIMLY LIT, but that doesn't detract from the smooth polished luster of its mahogany or the shine of the brass fittings and appointments throughout the place. It's obviously an expensive watering hole, and the prices are commensurate with the décor: high as hell. But I don't care. I'm flush these days.

The first double tastes like the nectar of the gods, and I almost miss the spectacular entrance of a woman dressed like, I swear, Elvira, Mistress of the Dark. I know it can't be the real Elvira, but this woman has the look down pat, from her floor-length slinky black dress slit near the top of her right thigh, to the push-up bra cleavage of two incredibly pale breasts. I was already feeling the painful strain of my abstinence, but this woman exacerbates it unbearably. I stare at her cleavage for ten minutes before I raise my eyes to meet hers. Amusement twinkles in her eyes and a sardonic smile lifts her lips when she sees that I've finally recognized her. Red. Fooled me again.

With a barely perceptible crook of her right forefinger, she beckons me over to her table, and I comply like a well-trained dog. It seems I have no pride at all when it comes to this woman.

She's moved her lips close to my ear and I can feel the heat of her breath. "Buy me a drink, and follow my lead." She places her hand high on my thigh, smooth as any Vegas hooker could have done it. The chills running up and down my spine and the pounding of my heart have absolutely nothing to do with fear or apprehension. My other physical reaction is entirely predictable. Hope she doesn't make me stand up—pun intended. Too late.

"Are you looking for a party?" Her voice is low and husky, but just audible enough for the gawping men in the next booth to hear her.

"I . . . uhhh . . . I . . . yeah." I haven't stuttered like this since I was a nervous kid. Her fingers clamp down painfully on my thigh, and her lips get closer to my ear. The tip of her tongue lashes out, and then her white teeth close on my earlobe.

"You could at least make it sound like you're enjoying this, dumbass." Her words aren't audible to the gawpers now; only I can hear them. She sounds vicious. Taking my hand and pressing it onto her belly, tantalizingly close to the bottom swell of one breast, she leans around and kisses me—a wet, probing kiss that raises my body temperature at least ten degrees.

"Now get me that drink."

I give the bartender a weak grin and raise two fingers. He's giving me a knowing smirk, and I know exactly what he's thinking. As much as I hate to admit it, under other circumstances, his assumption wouldn't be far off the mark. I've never paid for sex, a matter of personal pride and self-respect, but there is no doubt I would be tempted this time. Hell, forget *would* be. I *am* tempted. Not that it matters. Red will be back to Ice Princess mode as soon as we're out of sight of any onlookers.

She takes no more than a couple of sips from the drink. "Would you like to see my room, lover? It's really nice . . ." She's already standing, tugging at my hand, and I hurriedly pull out a twenty and toss it on the tabletop. After a moment's hesitation, I pull out another twenty and drop it next to my untasted second drink.

I'll give Red one thing: when she's in character, she goes whole hog. When we reach the elevator, she starts giggling as if I've said something endearingly funny and swings me against the wall while we're waiting for the door to open. Every achingly gorgeous curve of her body presses close to mine as her lips devour me. She grinds her hips against me and drags my hand up to the swell of her breast as an older couple watches us disapprovingly.

"Come on, Harold. We can wait for another elevator." The elder matron drags poor Harold away like an unruly child. I think she would have twisted his ear if he hadn't gone willingly.

I have an embarrassing and extremely visible reaction to Red's very real fake foreplay, but instead of ignoring it when we get into the elevator, Red backs into it and waggles her butt against me lasciviously, much to the amusement of the man already in the elevator. Before he gets off on the seventh floor, he gives me a sly wink. As soon as the elevator door closes behind him, Red jerks away as if she's been bitten by a rattler.

"I said act like you're enjoying it, asshole, not poke me with that thing. When are you going to start taking this business seriously?"

"Something tells me the love has gone out of our relationship . . ."

I can tell she's having a hard time suppressing a smile at my wisecrack by the way her lips crinkle up at the corners.

"We don't have that kind of relationship, Drew. Now get your mind back in the game. We need to have a serious conversation." Once the elevator doors open, she looks up and down the hallway and sees no one. "Come on, let's go to your room."

"I thought we were going to your room . . ."

"Don't be an ass, Drew." With that, she grabs my

hand and drags me down the hall to my suite. I open the door, and she flounces past me as if she owns the place. I freeze in the doorway, fascinated by the way her dress flutters around her ankles, her ass swaying when she walks. It is mesmerizing.

When I compose myself enough to shut the door and follow her inside, I am at a loss for words, but that doesn't matter. She has enough to say for both of us.

"How could you do this to me, Drew? I *vouched* for you! You said you would try harder. That you wouldn't screw up anymore. I even gave you a hint at what was supposed to be a surprise task, and you blew it the first damned day!"

I've never seen her this mad. Furious, she rips off the raven black bouffant wig and slams it onto the floor. I don't know what I expect next. Her eyes blaze through her blue contact lenses, her face contorts in rage, and her fists ball up as if she's going to pound me into dust. Which, I believe, she is entirely capable of doing.

"Damn you, Drew!" Before the phrase is out of her mouth, she is on me. Shoving me against the wall, she attacks me, but not the way I expected. The slit in her dress opens, exposing a dangerous amount of skin, and she hooks her leg behind my knee as her mouth ravages mine. My pulse skyrockets, and I make no effort at all to resist her. The kiss seems to last forever, but it's over way before I want it to be.

When our lips part, she is breathing as heavily as I am. "Damn you," she whispers. "I swear. One more time, Drew. Screw up just one more time, and I will have you bounced out of this program and off this tour. Do you understand me?"

She doesn't even give me time to answer. Shoving her hand into the bodice of her Elvira dress, she draws out another envelope and slaps it into my open hand.

"What's this for?"

"Don't get too excited. I gave half of it to the yokel who spotted you that first night. He'll keep his mouth shut, and you'd better do the same. This is a cushy gig for me, and I'm not going to let you fuck it up. I'm through taking chances on you. Straighten up, or get out now. This is it."

I look down at the envelope and see the indentation. I could ask her now. It would take one simple question. *What does this three mean?* But she's struggling to regain her professional composure, and I am speechless. Helpless to turn my eyes away, I watch her adjust her dress. A final tug, and she turns to me, her face an expressionless mask.

"The instructions for your next task are in the envelope. Last chance, Drew."

Second Show

The audience tonight seems to be the same mix as the last night in LA, so I'm feeling pretty confident with my material. I'm not even sweating as I walk onto the stage.

"I HAVE all but given up making decisions in my life. That's what I hate most about restaurants. There's too much decision process.

"Sometimes you go to a restaurant, it's late at night. You had a busy day. You just want that experience to be easy. Right?

"Don't give me choices. 'Hey, do you want to sit inside, outside? Here's a menu. It's 45 pages. Here's the wine list. There's about 700 to choose from. Here's the bread basket. You have 15 choices.'

"Too much, too much. I want a restaurant where I show up, I stand on an X, and they go, 'Come, sit here. You're having chicken. No dessert. Leave six bucks for the tip. Thank you.'

"Let me go this far. If there were an adult version of high chairs where you just sat down, they put random food in front of you, and when you were done, you knocked that shit off the tray and spent the rest of the time trying to sneak out, I would eat there every day.

"I know this has to bug my wife though, because now that I make fewer decisions, I store no information on my own hard drive," I say, tapping the side of my head. "I have now officially turned my wife into my own personal cloud. Any information I get, I don't store it here." I tap my head again. "I store it on *her* hard drive, and I just download that info when I need it. For example, if we go to a restaurant, I just look at her and ask, 'Do I like the Cesar salad here?' and she'll spit out the answer. 'Thank you, I will not be having the Cesar salad.'

"'Quick, how do I know this guy? Oh, he's my hairdresser? Thank you, and by the way, when's my next appointment?'

"But that's what marriage is. Give and take. I'll tell you this, my young friends, and don't go into a seizure. Did you know that when you get married, your wife moves in with you?

"And when she moves in with you, she'll make you get rid of everything you had prior to her? Neon signs you stole from bars, that beanbag you stress-pick beans out of, your *roommate*? Yeah, my wife made me get rid of my roommate. I miss Rob. Me and Rob had the greatest relationship in the entire world. Never once did Rob stick his toes under my butt because they were cold.

"Don't get me wrong. I love my wife, but I miss Rob. There were certain things I didn't need to worry about with Rob. Now, fellas, pay attention, because what I'm about to tell you is going to save your life. One day, you will buy a rug with your girl. She's going to pick out a rug, and this rug will go into your bathroom next to the bathroom tub. Now, listen to me. Because no joke, this *will* save your life. Under no circumstances is that rug ever, *ever* supposed to get wet.

"What you're supposed to do instead is stand in that shower until you are completely dry. You let life dry you off, because the towel hanging outside the shower can't get wet either. Everything you see in your bathroom is for guests who never visit. That's also why you have a guest bedroom where nobody has slept since you've owned that house. It's really just an expensive room for your cat to throw up in. An entire room of furniture and bedding picked out especially for guests who never come, and you walk by to find your cat with the comforter in her mouth.

"'What's up? Pretty nice room you've got in here. I appreciate the goose down duvet. And if you haven't figured it out yet, I've been pissing in that corner, too.'

"And I know what you're thinking. 'So what? I get a little bit of water onto the floor, and she steps in it.' But here's where you've got to see the bigger picture. You've got to backwards engineer this. Because you're right. There's nothing wrong with getting a little bit of water on the floor and her stepping into it. One time. But then she might step into it another time. And over the years, she might step into gallons of water and not *once* say anything to you. Except one day she'll hit that magic number when enough is enough, and she'll go ape shit. And here's the scary thing about it: your wife won't reveal what that number is. She doesn't even necessarily know. It's kind of like this. You can finish spreading peanut butter with a butter knife and set that knife in the sink. (You get zero credit for that knife making it into the sink, by the way. This is strictly pass/fail.) She will walk by, see that knife, lift it up, and wipe off the peanut butter, but when she does that, deep inside, she goes, 'Erh.' And then she will see it again and wipe it off. 'Erh.'

"And like a video game, the more knives she collects, the more powerful she becomes. And one day, she will go ape shit. Know what that is? *Dading dading dadidididing*," I sing while turning an invisible little crank. "Human jack-in-the-box."

"None of you have a good feeling in your stomach right now. Worst game in childhood history. They should literally call that game, 'Here kid, let's learn about anxiety.'

"Every time you do something that pisses off your girl, you're one *ding* closer to her going ape shit. And you'll know when it happens because her rage will not be proportional to the crime you committed. So if you ever find yourself going, 'What the fuck? I just left, what, I just left something on the table,' you've probably just hit your last *ding*.

"But here's my real advice. Every once in a while, you have to *make her* go off the chart crazy. You have to get that shit out of her system. You've got to ring up all your remaining *dings* at once so that last one doesn't catch you off guard.

"It's scary, I know, but here's what you do. Next time she's on the couch watching TV, get a Swiffer, and start poking her with it. You're going to start to sweat. It's a natural response. She is going to say, 'Quit it, knock it off.'

"At this point, try to remember, fear is in your brain. Remember the reason why you're doing this. You've got to get your girl to go crazy. Because if you let that shit build up, she may decide to kill you in your sleep.

"If you haven't seen your girl freak out in a while, fellas, chances are you've had a pillow over your face one or two nights. Lucky for you, she talked herself out of it. But don't kid yourself because it wasn't out of love. It was because she remembered you need to feng shui the living room tomorrow or you would be a dead man.

"That's another lesson, fellas. Never finish everything on your to do list. Keep some shit on there. That's your life insurance policy."

THE INSTRUCTIONS in the envelope are deliberately vague, and I'm wondering if Red decided to eliminate me after all. Even so, I find myself more caught up in my assignment than I am in my audience reaction—a first for me. I know I have to look for a chartreuse pin, but Red didn't give me the slightest clue as to the person who would be wearing it. She didn't even describe what kind of pin I'm supposed to look for. On the surface, it seems an impossible task, but I'm caught up in the game in spite of my misgivings.

The money has me even more puzzled. Why would Red risk her "cushy gig" by paying me after I screwed up? I could understand her paying the first tail hush money, if I could figure out why she is giving me a pass in the first place. What's more, I can't understand why half of my due compensation amounts to over two grand. I know I'm being lured into something that isn't kosher, if not outright illegal, but whoever devised this scheme obviously knew which of my buttons to push and how to push them. Diabolical. With Red, fast money, and the promise of fame as bait, I've been an easy mark.

I'm no longer certain I can or even *want* to extricate myself from whatever this is, but I'm going to find a way to manage a face-to-face with Todd. I've always trusted him, but now I'm curious as to how much he knew about this "side gig" when he pulled me into it. I can't escape the thought that *somebody* has me in their clutches, and I'm ashamed to admit that I don't mind it that much.

DUFFY CALLS these things "Meet and Greets." I don't really mind them. They're kind of an ego booster. Unlike the venues I played in my earlier days, the clubs we're playing now discourage hecklers. If an audience member gets too drunk to behave or too rowdy, they are politely escorted out the door. The only comedian on the tour discomfited by that is Bob Thomas. He seems to feel that if he doesn't piss *somebody* off, his act has been a failure. I think he likes to use hecklers as a foil for comic relief—a gimmick. Candace even hinted that Bob has paid people to act out before.

With an effort, I quash my misgivings and begin to focus on my assignment. After just a few weeks, I'm impressed at how much easier it is to split my attention between glib conversations with audience members and spotting a target. It's almost second nature.

I spot my target about three-quarters of the way

through the event. It's hard to keep the chagrin off my face when I realize I've been focused on women and skimming over men. I should've known better than to look for Red in a disguise, especially since she went to such lengths to be vague. My mark is a balding, fat man with a florid complexion. He's wearing an immaculately tailored and very conservative three-piece suit. The chartreuse lapel pin he's wearing sticks out like a whore in church, and I should've spotted it as soon as I walked onto the floor.

My adrenaline surges as I approach him with my hand extended in greeting. I don't know how I manage to maintain a pleasant smile; I'm nervous as hell, scared that I'm going to muff this and that Red is going to deep-six me. He takes my hand in both of his.

"Awesome, man. Really enjoyed the show!" The smile on his face doesn't touch his eyes, which are cold, gray, and glittery. When we shake hands, I expect to feel the smooth surface of another slip of paper, and I'm surprised when it doesn't happen. It shows on my face despite my efforts to keep it off.

"There you are, Ed!" A chubby woman in a garish print dress attaches herself to the fat man and begins gushing over my performance, but the effusiveness of her compliments doesn't touch her eyes either. I am instantly alert, and a little alarmed. Whatever these people are, they aren't fans. I have no idea what to expect next.

After another minute or two of mindless drivel, the woman's expression changes. She gives me a sour look, nudges the fat guy, and they move on, leaving me standing here feeling like an idiot. Either I've missed something, or there's someone else here wearing a chartreuse pin who I haven't found yet. That had to have been the wrong guy.

I'm in full on panic mode now, making my way nervously through the crowd looking for another chartreuse pin.

By the time it's all over and they're turning down the lights, I still haven't found my contact, and I'm about to hyperventilate. I lean against a wall by the exit, and I'm sweating bullets. Red is scrapping me after this, I have no doubt, and I can see all of my hopes and dreams going up in smoke. Red warned me not to fuck up again, and I have.

"They're gonna shitcan you, ain't they, boy?"

I turn around to see Ed standing in front of me with a sympathetic look on his face. I'm not sure what is going on, so my mind searches frantically for a way to stall him long enough to get my shit together.

"Excuse me?"

"Come on, boy! Nobody's watchin', an' nobody's close enough ta hear us."

His Southwestern drawl is thick enough to cut with a dull butter knife, much more pronounced than it had been earlier.

"You screwed the pooch on this one, didn't ya?"

"I . . . I'm not sure what you mean . . ."

Ed's face screws up into a look of disgust. "Shee-it son! I'm feelin' kinda sorry for ya right now, an' I'm tryin' ta help ya. Ethel wants ta jist get back ta the house an' fergit about ya, an' I kin see where she's comin' from, but I feel plumb sorry fer ya. These folks play hardball son, an' that ain't no laughin' matter. It's serious. Gittin' on their bad side? Well, that ain't funny either."

He shivers, like he's remembering something horrible. What have I gotten myself into?

"Now listen good, sonny, cause Ethel's waitin', an' I ain't wantin' ta piss her off any more'n she already is. I'm gonna say my piece, an' then I'm gonna high-tail it out ta the truck afore she figgers out what I done. The newspaper, son. Remember the damn *newspaper*! If you'da read today's paper, you woulda known you was s'posed ta say somethin' ta us about ostriches, and I was s'posed ta give ya this."

He hands me a key with a tag on it and then glances around to see if anyone has seen him give it to me.

"It's at the damn bus station, son. Now git!"

IT'S STUPID, I know, but I'm hoping Red is in my room when I get back up there. I ought to know better. The suite is empty. The pangs of disappointment aren't bitter, but they sting anyway. It's just as well, though. Tonight has been a disaster. I kick myself mentally for forgetting the newspaper bit. I am supposed to read the personals section in the biggest local newspaper before every gig in Tucson, but it totally slipped my mind. Red told me it was just for practice, but she warned that newspapers would become essential in the days to come. She even mentioned paying specific attention to a day when "aardvark" and "bastille" appeared in the same ad. I thought she was pulling my leg.

THE POST-IT IS STUCK to the inside wall of a locker in the Greyhound bus station on East 12th Street. If Ed hadn't given me the key, I would have been in deep shit tonight. I still may be. Kicking myself, I grab a paper from the rack in the bus station and read the personals before returning to the hotel. I find it in the sole column, plain as day. "Aardvark" and "bastille" in the same ad.

I CONSOLE myself with a beer and a can of cashews from the mini-bar and sit down at the table before taking the Post-it note out of my pocket. Another OTP cipher. Five lines this time. I have to find the key, and I have no doubt it won't be so easy to find. She would have waited until I was onstage to conceal it this time, and she was really pissed when she left. I'm going to pay for that. Worse, if she talks to Ed or Ethel, she's gonna dropkick me into next week, if not outright abandon me.

It takes all night to find it. I swear I look

everywhere, checking my luggage, my shaving kit, behind the faux art on the walls, beneath the sink in the bathroom, and every nook and cranny in the suite. Nothing. I'm really getting pissed at Red by 7 a.m., when I stop to make myself a pot of coffee.

I'm exhausted, and I'm sleepy, but I'm not giving up. I decide to make my coffee and start over at the beginning. Not happy.

I'm numb all over, and my arms and legs move woodenly as I slowly head to the coffee basket. I pour the rest of my water bottle into the reservoir and rip open the coffee packet. When I turn it over to dump the filter pack into the machine, another paper falls out with it.

The damn key.

I'm angry, but I can take the hint. She *wanted* me to spend all night looking for it. She hid it in something I wouldn't use until morning to make sure her punishment was delivered.

I don't bother making the coffee. I'm not tired anymore, and my eyelids no longer feel like they are lined with sand.

MORE COMFORTABLE WITH the procedure now, I manage the decryption in short order. The message is enigmatic, and it takes me more time to figure out what the message means that it did to decrypt it in the first place. The first three blocks of five characters turn out to be the name of a local private mailbox service. (Try figuring that out without the aid of the Internet!) The next few blocks turn out to be a confirmation number, each character separated by the letter X. That took some time as well. It is noon before I get dressed to go out. My ass is dragging, and I know I need sleep for my performance tonight at eight, but I'm too excited to wait any longer.

The cashier is a jovial, porcine man in his mid-thirties. He cheerfully hands over a manila envelope with my name and the confirmation number written in magic marker on the front. Despite feeling a little foolish and paranoid, I tuck the envelope inside my shirt and return to the hotel suite to open it. Because of how badly I got stung in San Diego, my little trip is punctuated by sudden stops, which I use to scan the sidewalk crowds for a tail. Out of what is probably an excess of caution, I circumnavigate the block around the hotel twice, continuing my periodic stops before entering the service entrance. I feel like an idiot, but at least I'm almost certain no one is following me.

Once the door to my suite is closed, I tear open the manila envelope and withdraw an unmarked plain white envelope . . . but something is wrong with this one. It doesn't feel right. I reach for the X-Acto knife and slit the bottom of the envelope. I can't see any sign of an imprint on this one, but I'll check it later.

The only thing inside the white envelope is a single brass key with a number stamped on it—just like the one Ed passed to me. I feel my pulse rate rise, but this time it has nothing to do with excitement or fear. I am pissed.

EAST 12TH STREET. Again. The locker is easy to locate, but instead of going directly to it, I walk over to the concession area and buy an exceptionally lousy cup of black coffee and another newspaper, which I then carry over to a bench with a clear view of both the locker and the main entrance. Sleep tugs at the corners of my eyes, but I'm not ready to give up. Scanning the crowd for more than an hour, I don't see anyone scoping out the locker or paying undue attention to me. I read the personals section, but there's no "aardvark" this time. I don't even bother looking for "bastille."

Even though I've spotted no untoward observers, I'm nervous as I approach the locker and insert the key. My self-confidence has taken a terrible blow, and my imagination is working overtime. I keep expecting to feel a tap on my shoulder from either a cop telling me I'm under arrest for something I don't even know about, or Red telling me that I've been followed and I'm out on my ass. Neither happens. Inside the locker is the plain white envelope I have come to expect. The envelope instantly disappears inside my shirt and I walk away, the key still in the lock.

INSIDE MY SUITE, I take the time to examine the envelope and then dust the corners even though I know what I'll find. At this point, I'm probably just making sure I'm not crazy.

There is five thousand dollars in the envelope this time, and once again the cold fingers of fear tickle my brain. So far, I've swallowed the assertions that this side job is a matter of industrial espionage involving enormous sums, but this much cash, dumped in my lap so quickly and for so little effort, smacks of the drug business. I need to talk to Todd . . . and soon.

I make the call from the lobby telephone, following the instructions Duffy gave me and using an anonymous prepaid phone card. All I get is his voicemail, and I leave a message telling him that I'm concerned about this side work and that I need to see him in person as soon as possible.

STILL GROGGY from my long day yesterday, I stumble from my bed and throw on the complimentary terry cloth robe provided by the hotel. Who the hell can be knocking on my door at this ungodly hour? I'm yawning, and my hair looks like a flock of starlings nested in it overnight.

To my surprise, Jason Keene, my agent, is standing in front of the door to my suite, dressed to the nines and looking like a fashion plate right off the cover of GQ. My heart drops into my stomach. This is where I get the bad news, I guess. At least I don't have to face Red's wrath.

With a grin that would light up a cave, he brushes past me and takes a seat at the small table where the coffee pot sits. Housekeeping hasn't come by yet, so the basket that held the packets of coffee is empty, even though the bowl of creamer, sweeteners, and swizzle sticks is still full to overflowing. Jason, never one to mince words, skips the preliminaries and cuts straight to the chase.

"You're fucking up, Drew." His smile is fake and cold. "You're messing up the best gig you're ever going to get. The magic money pool is in serious jeopardy of drying up."

He doesn't have to say it. Todd ratted me out. He must have told Jason about my panicked call last night, or worse, Red found out and told him about the newspaper fiasco. Seems like I can't hide anything from her.

"Drew, listen to me. You've got my personal assurance that everything you're doing is legit and aboveboard. You're not guilty of breaking any laws."

He shakes his head, and I realize, in a moment of surreal unreality, that I have never seen a single hair on his head out of place.

"I shouldn't have to remind you that CTA is a very powerful force in this industry. They can make big things happen for you. Really big things. Specials on HBO. Netflix. *Vidxy*. You just need to shut the hell up, do what you're told, and take the money, Drew."

He seems almost affable as he speaks, but there is a hard line of deadly seriousness beneath every word. I know a threat when I hear one. His smile transforms into a broad, false grin. "Be a smart guy, Drew. Do the right thing." He winks—the guy actually *winks* at me like in one of those 1950s comics. "If there's anything you need, and I really do mean *anything at all*, just ask Mandy. She's a real trooper that girl. She'll take care of you."

"Mandy? Who the hell is Mandy?"

"Amanda, of course. Don't tell her I called her that. She hates when I call her Mandy, but I do it to make sure she knows her place."

Could he mean Red? If he does, he's just pissed me off a hell of a lot more.

His grin is gone, replaced by a thin, hard smile. "You need her, Drew. She's your lifeline. If it weren't for her covering for you, I wouldn't be here, and you would be back in Detroit flipping burgers and looking for your next stand-up gig. Stick close to her, Drew. She likes you. And remember, just do what you're told and take the money."

I watch him stand up, check the creases of his trousers with his thumb and forefinger, and then, I swear, shoot his cuffs like a James Bond character. He leaves without saying another word or even glancing back over his shoulder. Arrogant bastard. He doesn't even close the door behind him.

Totally stunned, I stagger over to the door and shut it, then make my way to the bathroom to take a shower.

I'm not even able to focus on Jason's implied threats. The only thing I can think about is his crack about making sure Red knows her place.

At least this encounter has answered one of my pressing questions. Jason knows a *lot* more about what's going on than I thought he did. Hell, he's in up to his neck. I'm not even sure he's not in charge.

The rest of my time in Tucson, I don't hear a word from Todd. Or from Red. Maybe she doesn't know about my phone call after all.

CHAPTER TEN

DENVER, COLORADO

First Show

"I REMEMBER when I was in college, we used to play this game called Donkey Kong where one of us would start at the bottom of our apartment complex steps and run up them, and the other person would take kegs or half barrels and try to bash the other down. Right?

"You fellas in your twenties, I've got some bad news. That game I played no problem over twenty years ago? My body *remembers*. And everything you're doing to your bodies right now?" I point around at the younger men in the audience. "Your body will remember, too."

"I remember taking a fire extinguisher to the arm once. I just kind of fell. I popped up and was like, 'Man, nothing happened.' About two weeks ago, I'm blow drying my hair, and my blow-dry-my-hair muscle shit out on me. I'm like, 'What the hell?' And my body was like, 'Remember that fire extinguisher? No? Well, *I* do.'

"And right now, fellas, all of your plumbing works pretty good. You can drink a bunch of beer, start to take a piss in the street, think you see a cop, and shut that stream down dry. Right? Full blast, you can shut the stream off, throw it back in your pants completely dry. Full blast, shut it off, back in your pants completely dry. Now you're thinking, 'Well, Drew, isn't it always going to work that way?'

"No. Let's take a journey. During this trip, you're going to develop some Wikileaks, and one day you're going to be pissing, and you're going to have this conversation with yourself: 'Okay, I've shaken it an obscene amount of times, so I'm going to leave it out of my fly and walk around for a few minutes.'" I prance around for a second like I haven't a care in the world and then look down at my fly with an exaggerated look of shock on my face.

"Now in your brain, you're going to be like, 'There's no way there's anything left.' And you're going to throw it back in your pants. Two minutes later, especially if you're wearing khaki pants, there it will be. That half-dollar piss mark right on your crotch. And, to top that off, you'll have to have this bullshit conversation with your wife:

"'Do you piss your pants?'

"'What?'

"'I just did laundry. It's disgusting. You have piss stains all over your underwear.'

"'Are we seriously talking about my underwear?'

"'I'm not making fun of you. I just want to know. Are you peeing, and then you just pull up your pants midstream? Like, why do you not completely empty it?'

"Ladies, don't ever talk to your guy about his underwear. His underwear has nothing to do with you. And trust me, ladies, as hygienic as you are, there has been a moment you're unaware of when your guy has walked past your underwear, and he had questions. But you know what? He was a gentleman and didn't say anything to you. He walked down the hall, looked down at your underwear, and just went, 'Yikes.' But that's all he did. He knew it wasn't your first rodeo. You'd get it cleaned. Jumping into a conversation about your underwear wasn't going to speed things along.

"That's usually when you ladies are like, 'Let's make love,'" I say in a mocking falsetto, eyelashes batting.

"And that's why out of nowhere, your man has zero interest. 'I was thinking we don't kiss enough. Maybe we should just kiss. I don't feel like we're *connected* because we don't kiss. Let's just kiss.'

"'In the meantime, when's the last time you've seen a doctor, because I'd love to know you have a clean bill of health.'"

TONIGHT IS the first of a three-night gig here in Denver, and I'm still uneasy. I haven't heard from anybody since Jason's visit. Neither Duffy nor Red (I'm not going to refer to her as Mandy or Amanda, because I don't know if she's aware of Jason's visit, and I am not going to risk getting my ass kicked) has made an appearance, and while I got the impression from Jason that I'm still in this program, I'm not absolutely certain nothing has changed. Nobody has said a word about my newspaper fuck-up, so that's still hanging over my head, too. I open the *Denver Post* to the personals section and read it again, very carefully, just in case I missed 'aardvark'. I'm not about to let that happen again.

The hell of it is, before Jason's visit and the newspaper debacle, there was still a tiny, niggling doubt in my mind as to whether I wanted to continue the training. It has become crystal clear that I am a pawn in a much larger game. But it's a game I need. Sure, maybe some comedians make it all away to the top completely on their own, but I don't believe there are many of them. Everybody gets a boost from somewhere. A benefactor in the industry, a cousin or distant relative. Maybe even from politicians. The fact that I never stumbled onto CTA's little operation is a function of my own naïveté. I either didn't see it, or I turned a blind eye to it. It doesn't matter anymore. I see that my future is defined by CTA now. My earlier assessment was spot on. I'm in all the way, and what's worse, I'm eager to continue. Fame, bright lights, and money in my pocket. Everything dreams are made of.

For the first time since I started this tour, I'm not thrilled about visiting with the audience, but I put on my best stage smile and do it anyway. It doesn't stop me from wondering about Duffy and Red. I'm exhausted by the time I get through with the meet and greet, and I decide that what I want more than anything else is to go to the hotel bar and get drunk out of my mind. The problem with that is twofold. It's a rare occasion for me to get drunk, and alcohol tends to loosen my mouth—not a good thing for a guy in my position. The other problem is Red. No matter how hard I try, I will never be able to get the image of her in Elvira's dress out of my head. Every time I enter a bar for the rest of my life, I'm going to see her. I'm pretty sure that's not a good thing. I can manage to be stupid enough without adding alcohol and lust to the mix. The best idea for me would be to go up to my suite and put myself to bed. Time enough to worry about Duffy or Red tomorrow.

I must be getting better at this, because I notice the tiny strip of tape I placed on my door jamb is crinkled and twisted.

I'm not sure exactly what to expect, but seeing Red stretched out in my bed, one bare leg peeking out from beneath the sheets, is not it. That's not to say I'm unhappy about it. But as bad as I want to see her again, I am filled with dread. Is this where she fires me?

Her denim jacket, jeans, and boots are puddled on the floor beside the bed, and in spite of my (continuously failing) intentions to keep things on a professional level between us, I am aroused. I don't even think, I simply sit on the edge of the bed beside her and reach out one trembling hand to touch her hair.

She has the lightning reaction of a striking snake. Before my hand even grazes her, she is sitting up in the bed, the fingers of her left hand twisted in my hair and her right hand holding a knife against my throat.

"Dumbass."

The knife makes a distinct click as she closes it and tucks it into the lacy red bra she wears. My heart is still pounding so badly from the scare she threw into me that I barely notice the only other thing she is wearing is a flimsy pair of matching panties when she hops out of bed.

"You should know better than to sneak up on me by now, Drew."

"And you should know better than to climb into my bed half naked by now. I love being teased, but I can only take so much of it."

I feel a little of my confidence coming back. After all, I've learned a little bit about her that she doesn't know I know. I'm not naïve enough to think I have the upper hand with her now, but if she doesn't know I got help from Ed, I'm in a better position than I thought. I'm going to pretend nothing has happened and hope for the best. This calls for a little bravado I don't really feel.

"I wasn't teasing you. I was tired for Christ's sake. I meant to take a short nap during your show. I had no intention of being asleep when you got here."

She's snarling, her lips curled in disgust. She knows I'm distracted by her curves and probably fully aware of what's going through my mind. Given today's politically correct climate, I'm absolutely, one hundred percent certain that I could go to jail just for thinking what I'm thinking, so I keep my mouth shut.

"Make some coffee, Drew." She says it with a smirk, and I know she must be pleased with herself for hiding that key somewhere I'd take eons to find. "I need to take a quick shower, and then we need to talk."

Uh oh.

When she does that woman thing, somehow inverting her hands and putting them behind her back to unfasten her bra, I do something totally out of character for me. I turn away and go to the kitchenette to make coffee. There is no doubt in my mind that if I see her naked, I will never get any sleep tonight. Ha! As if that were the most dangerous thing that could happen . . .

The last of the coffee is dripping into the pot before it occurs to me that Red might be playing me. Jason has been my agent for years, and I thought I knew him well. I've only known Red for a few weeks. Is it possible? Is all this teasing—all this off-again on-again passion—a show put on for my benefit? Is she cold-blooded enough to tie me up in knots just because Jason told her to? Is she about to lower the boom on me over the newspaper bit now?

Suddenly, I've lost my taste for coffee. I don't even bother to take the sanitary wrappers off the coffee cups. I just fold my hands and wait patiently for Red to finish her shower. There's a sour taste in my mouth and a hot ball of anger in my gut, even though I'm not wholly convinced that she's playing me. Just the possibility that she could be toying with my emotions so callously is enough to make my blood boil. I have to fight to suppress my feelings before she comes out. I know I need to be clearheaded for whatever comes next, and I know that's not going to happen if I'm thinking with the wrong head or wallowing in self-pity. I have to remind myself again that I have a new set of goals. I cannot allow my desire for this woman to destroy my chances.

Red walks out of the bathroom and shrugs into the formfitting denim jacket, not bothering to fasten the buttons in the front and leaving the fetching red lace bra exposed. I force my eyes away from the tantalizing view and concentrate on unwrapping one of the coffee cups. Sitting down across from me and leaning over to reach for the coffee pot, Red lets her jacket fall open, giving me an even better view. With a massive effort, I lock eyes with her instead of staring at the creamy upper slopes of the breasts threatening to spill out of her bra. A shadow of a smile crosses her lips, but it's gone in a split second, and she's back to business. She pours coffee into the cup I unwrapped and sets the pot back down.

"I don't know why they put these cheap two-cup coffee makers in these suites, considering the astronomical prices they charge. You can never get two full cups out of them."

I have to draw on an inner strength I wasn't aware I possessed to keep from breaking eye contact with her, but somehow I manage. "What have you got for me?"

I know that's a double entendre, but the urge to needle her is too strong for me to resist. To her credit, she doesn't react at all.

"This next task will be the toughest one yet, Drew. You're getting better, but you're still not quite up to standard."

She lifts the coffee cup in both hands and takes a sip. Does she know or not? Her eyes close and the smile that comes to her lips seems genuine, but that doesn't matter to me anymore. She breaks eye contact first, and the tickle of a small thrill of victory washes over me.

"You're going to construct an OTP all by yourself tonight. Do it the way I taught you. Write your message out first, then break it down into blocks of five characters. Pick a character that is not used in the message as a spacer. Remember, the choice of spacer character is absolutely critical. Got it?"

"Got it."

"Good. It's going to take a little time, so I'm going to order some nachos and a beer from room service while you work, then I'm going to take another nap. I'm exhausted."

I'm so curious about what she's been doing that has her so tired that I don't even object when she uses the landline in my room to call room service. She's having it billed to my room, but I couldn't care less. No matter how suspicious I am of her, she is the goose that laid the golden egg. I don't have to worry about room service charges anymore. I'm also a little insulted that she would think it would take me so long to create an

OTP key that she would have time to eat and then take a nap while I do it.

To my chagrin, she turns out to be right. The nachos smell good, but I never look up as she eats them. When I pause my cipher efforts, her clothes are lying on the floor beside my bed again, and she is fast asleep.

"ARE YOU FINISHED?"

I hand her the cipher key, but it's not neat and precise like the ones she has given me in the past. The message, with its number blocks, is much cleaner, even though I had to make several erasures to make everything work. There are a lot more erasures on the key, but it's legible.

Red scrutinizes the key and her lower lip curls in mild distaste, but it takes her no time to decipher my message. It's a little embarrassing to me that she can do it without pencil and paper like I have to. The woman has a remarkable memory.

"Did you keep a copy of the key for yourself?"

"Of course I did, I'm not stupid."

She holds out her hand, palm up.

"Then give it to me, jackass, and you better hope it's cleaner and more legible than this one. How the hell do you expect your contact to use this thing?"

My teeth click audibly as my mouth snaps shut. She is absolutely right, and once again I have fouled up. With as meek an expression on my face as I can manage, I hand over the copy that I made for myself and take back the one with all the erasures and corrections on it.

"Pay attention, Drew. I'm only going to give you these instructions one time, and then I'm out of here. The only way you will ever see me or Duffy again is if you complete this assignment flawlessly. If you flub this one, you will not be permitted to board the flight to Kansas City. You will be given a ticket to Detroit, and your contract with the tour will be terminated."

I'm sitting here horrified because I know I have no other option. It's clearer to me than ever before how much responsibility and control CTA has over my gig here. Even if I decide not to go any further with CTA and go back to my regular life, there's no telling how they would react. Would I still get kicked off the tour? Would I even be able to get gigs? I'm an idiot for taking so long to realize it, but I'm being held hostage in this deal. If I want to keep doing comedy, I need to keep working with CTA.

"Are you with me so far?" Red asks.

She has to know I'm putting the pieces together. But I also know she is in absolute earnest about what she's saying. All I can do is nod my head like an idiot.

Red sighs. "You have two more shows here in Denver. Perform your shows as scheduled, but starting tomorrow morning, get out and about. Daytime and nighttime. Go shopping, go to a library, catch a street fair. I don't care, just get out. At some point, you will be approached by an individual who will identify themselves to you by using the words 'arachnid' and 'toluene' in the same sentence. 'Arachnid' and 'toluene.' No, Drew. Don't write them down. Remember something important for one damned time."

She's angry now, and I drop the number two pencil in my hand like a scolded schoolboy.

"Your contact will recognize you by this. Carry it under your left arm." She lifts the *Denver Post* off the table and makes a show of folding it into a rectangle while staring into my eyes with a look I can't interpret but that sends chills down my spine. Does she know? "Your acknowledgment has to be 'pterodactyl,' or the pass will not be attempted."

"You're joking . . ."

Red acts as if I haven't responded.

"You will execute a flawless brush pass, and you will find someplace private to decrypt the message. The message itself will be another set of instructions guiding you to another contact, one who will pass you another coded message. Only when you comply with the second message will you have completed this task successfully." Red gives me a look that is almost sorrowful. "Good luck, Drew."

I am worried sick.

Third Show

"I'm amazed by my dogs. I have two German Shepherds, and I can't believe how fast they make decisions. That's how I'm trying to live my life. I'm sick of my whole life being, 'Well, if I do this, then what if this happens? What if that?' Blah blah blah. I spend more time preparing for worst case scenarios than it would take to actually deal with that scenario if it happened. Do you ever see how fast your dog makes a decision? If I'm outside with my dogs, and a squirrel runs across the yard, my dogs don't go, 'Hmmm, should we? Do *you* want to?'

"'I don't know, do *you*?'

"'I don't know. I mean, I just don't feel like it today. I mean, I will if you do. I just, I'm not feeling confident right now. I think if I ever caught the squirrel, then I would have to stop bitching about my life. I think I enjoy not catching the squirrel and self-sabotaging so I can bitch about my life, because I enjoy that more than actually doing anything.'

"My dogs don't do that. If I ask them a question, they answer instantly.

"'You guys want to go for a walk?'

"'Fuck yes! Fuck yes! Let's go! Let's go! That would be awesome! Let's go. Let's go. Let's go. We're going to go right to the right. The second we get outside, we're going to go to the right. I just want to let you know. There's a dog a couple houses down, I want to see what that bitch says when I show up face-to-face with her. Let's go. You're tough from behind a fence, aren't you, sweater bitch? Let's go. Let's go. Talking, I'm a German Shepherd. You don't talk to me that way.'

"My dogs don't want to do something? I don't gotta figure that out, right? They hear water running in the bathroom, they think they're getting a bath, and their ears shoot behind their head, they drop low, and they start crawling away. 'We are so low, there's no way he can see us. Yeah and we're moving so slow, this is too slow for him to even see if we just go like this.'

"But that's how I know if my dogs did something wrong. If I walk into the room, even if it looks fine, if they both get up and start that crawl, I'm like, 'What did you guys do?'

"They're like, 'Yeah, hey, so the trash fell, just wanted to let you know before we leave. Trash fell. We don't have hands so we couldn't help pick shit up. So we just started eating everything and hoped that was cool. But then we were like, eh, maybe we shouldn't have eaten it, so we threw it up in the guest bedroom. Hopefully, that works out for you. Gotta go now. Bye.'"

MY BIT FELT a little flat tonight, but maybe that's because I'm a nervous wreck. No one approached me after last night's show, and even though I went to an open-air market this morning and spent the afternoon downtown at the Museum of Contemporary Art, no one has approached me with the codewords. My patience is wearing thin. Restless and irritable, I rush through the meet and greet and go back to my hotel suite to change. Maybe I haven't been out enough.

I strip off my clothes and toss them on the bed, then throw on the only pair of jeans I brought with me. Lived-in is the best way I can describe them, but they comfort me in a way I could never explain to another living soul. A t-shirt, a hoodie, and a pair of athletic shoes complete my transformation. I'm going out on the street to give my unknown contact another shot at me. If nothing else, I can practice watching for a tail.

Funny, but before this tour and this weird-ass side job came along, I believed I was a dedicated professional. Now I understand that I've been fooling myself all along. It's time to put some serious effort into my career . . . or should I say careers? The idea of having fame as a comedian while simultaneously maintaining the lifestyle of a corporate James Bond–type appeals to me in a major way. Ever since I was a little kid, I wanted to be the very best at something—anything. This is my chance, but it's going to take an enormous amount of effort and concentration to take advantage of it. The first thing I'm going to have to do is get my mind off of Red's physical attributes and focus on developing the skill set CTA's shadowy clients demand of an operative. *Operative.* That's how I have to start thinking of myself now.

The sensation that I'm being watched hits me before I manage to walk a full block, though I can't spot an obvious tail. Slowing down my pace, I change direction and begin to wander aimlessly, keeping a sharp eye out. Doesn't take long at all to spot her. It's a woman, a little frowzy, totally nondescript. It amazes me the way Red has found so quickly another person to play her little game. How in the hell does she do it all by herself. *Is she doing it by herself?*

I increase my pace until the distance between me and the woman decreases to a block. Ducking down an alley, I kick it into high gear and begin to run as fast as I can. Looking over my shoulder, I can see no sign of the woman, so without any hesitation I dive into the top of an open recycling dumpster. Crouching down inside it, I'm grateful that there only seems to be paper and cardboard boxes inside. After a short while, my breath coming in short gasps, I hear hesitant footsteps in the alley and hold my breath.

Sweating freely inside my hoodie, and really worried that I'm going to make noise of some kind, I wait until I hear the footsteps moving away from my dumpster. After they're gone, I force myself to wait a full thirty minutes before peering out over the lip of the dumpster. I experience a moment's panic when I realize I've dropped my paper, and though it takes me a minute or so, I find it. Outside the dumpster, I allow myself a small grin. I'm getting better at this shit.

Denver is so well lit that it could just as well be daytime. There's not as much foot traffic now, but there's still plenty of people about. I'm not just passing people the way I used to, I'm *seeing* them now. There is no way I can commit the appearance of every person to memory, but I'm learning to spot similarities and that leads to recognition when I spot them a second time. I read somewhere that memory is like a muscle, and the way to make a muscle grow stronger is to exercise it.

That's what I'm doing now, and not just with people, but with street names, store names, and signs. I may not remember everything, but I'm taking in so much more about my surroundings than I ever have before.

The techniques for spotting a tail must become second nature, but they can't take on a recognizable pattern. I have to vary the distances I move before stopping, and I have to make a concerted effort to keep from simply turning around and looking behind me. Reflective surfaces, especially storefront windows, are excellent devices for spotting what's behind you. Windows aren't the only resource, though; any reflective surface will serve. Polished stone, the mirrors on parked cars, even a shiny paint job on a freshly washed vehicle will work just as well. The windshield of a parked taxi provides me with my first hit of the night —a tall, bearded man wearing a western style Carhartt parka about forty feet behind me.

He's staring at me, but he keeps on walking and doesn't turn around. Even though he's passed by me without looking, I make a serious effort to remember the style and color of his coat. Not much danger of forgetting that bushy brown beard though.

THE BEARDED MAN still hasn't approached me by the time I decide to go back to the hotel and get some sleep. When I'm a few blocks away, I spot him leaning against a lamp post, but I keep walking, careful not to break stride. Just as I'm passing by him, I hear him speak one word.

"Arachnid."

I stop in my tracks, rubbing my hands together for warmth and looking up at the sky. "What did you say?"

"Arachnid. I've been trying for hours to figure out how to use the words arachnid and toluene in the same sentence, but I'll be damned if I can figure it out. Heh! Guess I just did."

I'm startled. I don't know what I expected, but it wasn't this guy. Is it possible that Red is using rank amateurs? People off the street willing to perform a task for a few bucks? Have I gotten the wrong impression and is this whole program some cockeyed scheme of Jason's? That's a sobering thought. I somehow manage to keep a straight face and a conversational tone.

"Somebody said if I came down here this time of night, I might get to see a pterodactyl. Have you seen one?"

I stick my hand out to shake his.

Beard laughs. "Dude, that was slick! I was even more curious about how you would find a way to use that word than I was about how to work my two words into the conversation."

He looks down at my newspaper and then at my outstretched hand.

"Oh, sorry!"

He reaches into his pocket, pulls out a crumpled note, and clumsily palms it before taking my hand in his.

The note, wadded up, is difficult to palm, but I manage to get the transfer accomplished without dropping it. Only then do I notice his pupils are dilated and his hands are unsteady. The wind changes and I get a whiff of his clothing. He's high as a kite. Hope this guy got his money up front. If Red finds out he's been smoking weed he'll be lucky to get a dime from her. She can't hang this one on me though. I was perfect.

APPARENTLY I REALLY AM LEARNING. Decrypting the wadded-up cipher only takes a few minutes. Under a streetlight a few blocks from where I left the grinning bearded guy, I figure out the abbreviations of the decoded message. It tells me that if I haven't messed up, I have already seen my next contact. There is also an address where my next contact can be found . . . and a specific time to meet. Glancing down at my watch, I see that I have less than ten minutes before the time listed in the cipher. If I run, I might actually be able to make it.

I'm not in the best of shape. Touring, late hours, irregular sleep and meals, and regular alcohol intake—none of that is conducive to good physical condition. I'm going to have to start working out. I should've figured that out after Red trashed me in the barn back in Vail.

The address is a storefront less than half a mile from where I met my first contact. Even so, by the time I arrive I have to bend over and rest my hands on my knees, wheezing and out of breath.

"That's a shame," says a voice from the shadows. I don't have to see her face to know my contact is smirking. It's hard to raise my head enough to see clearly, but I can see well enough to know who she is.

"I don't know what this younger generation is coming to." The woman I hid from in the dumpster is now wearing a parka and one of those silly knit caps with ear flaps and dangling pompoms.

"A young man like you, puffing like a locomotive climbing a steep grade after a little run like that?"

"Hey, I've never been a runner. Besides, I save my strength for when I really need it."

"If you're going to stay in this business, sonny boy, you'd best put some effort into getting in shape. I've been doing this for a lot of years, and I can tell you from experience that you never know what's going to happen next."

The look on her face is almost gleeful as she reaches out her hand and taps the folded paper. I stick my hand out to shake with her but instead of handing me another note, she places a wooden cube about the third the size of a Rubik's cube in my palm.

"What's this?"

She cackles like a witch on one of those old black-and-white Halloween movies. With that, she's gone—and moving fast. She's completely out of sight before I even catch my breath.

BACK IN THE SUITE, I set the small wooden cube in the center of the dinette table and then turn on the overhead lights. The cube is made of a dozen or more interlocking pieces of unvarnished wood. There are alpha characters on four sides of the cube, in groupings that strongly suggest that they are parts of words. Obviously there is a message here, and just as obviously the puzzle has to be disassembled and then reassembled in such a manner as to unscramble the message. I think I've seen something like this before, but it wasn't so small, and the writing wasn't so tiny. It takes four hours of disassembling and reassembling the cube before I finally manage to figure it out.

> *Drew,*
> *If you are reading this, you have finally*
> *established that you are worthy of further*
> *training. Solving this puzzle proves that you have*
> *the necessary skills to proceed to the next level. We*
> *will talk further in Kansas City, where I can give*
> *you more information about our project. Take a*
> *break, and enjoy your rest. You've earned it. Your*
> *envelope is in your hotel safe.*

CHAPTER ELEVEN

KANSAS CITY, MISSOURI

IT'S the third straight night at the club in Westport, Kansas City's entertainment district, and I've been knocking them dead every night. The audiences have been crazy about me, laughing their heads off at everything I say. I should be the happiest guy on earth, but I'm not. I'm on pins and needles waiting to hear from Red. I haven't heard from her since Denver. The message on the cube was so promising and, well, friendly. I grin to myself. There's always a small part of me that thoroughly rejects professionalism when it comes to Red.

Kansas City has an extraordinary number of public fountains, and my cabbie is as proud of them as if he owned them personally. The ride back to the Westin Crown Center takes me past more than two hundred of the most incredible fountains I've ever seen, every one of them lit up for the night. The last fountain on the impromptu tour is an impressive modern one by the hotel in Westin Crown Center Square.

The tour spared no expense on this K.C. stop, putting me up in an extravagant suite overlooking the best part of the city. The glass elevator in the atrium overlooks a waterfall, no joke, that cascades down from near the roof. Every time I get on, I get dizzy looking out at the spectacle. Even so, I can't even force myself to close my eyes. It's gorgeous.

By the time I run my key card through my room's reader, I'm tired, but it's a good tired. I feel a brief surge of anticipation as I enter the suite, but it quickly drains out of me when I see that Red isn't here. Uncharacteristic melancholy washes over me, and I make my way over to the drapes concealing the balcony and open them to stare out on the city lights. I know in my head that my feelings for Red are absolutely not in my best interest, but it seems my heart isn't the least concerned with what my head has to say. On a whim, I go to the bedroom and open my suitcase, removing the little Chinese wood puzzle and carrying it out to the dinette table.

I've left it in pieces, so I have to reassemble it to read the message again, which is really kind of stupid because I've committed Red's words to memory. The cube is actually a marvelous little piece of engineering, with seventeen oddly shaped pieces of wood that can be assembled in several different ways. It was a real challenge to reassemble the first time to make the message was readable.

It's much easier to assemble the right way this time. I guess practice makes perfect. I sit for several minutes, rereading the message and turning the puzzle over in my hands before my stomach starts to grumble. I was too nervous to eat before the show, and I try not to eat late at night, so room service is out of the question. A can of nuts and a soft drink will be enough to stop the grumbles, and the minibar is well-stocked.

As soon as I open the door, I spot a plain index card. The card's presence means Red got in here without disturbing the indicators I left on the door. She taught me the techniques, it wouldn't have been any trouble for her to circumvent them. I've got to find a way to refine those methods so that no one can get around them.

Snatching it from its resting place, I quickly turn it over.

Spot me tonight. Will give you some answers. Not all but some. Maybe more.

Maybe more. Images spring up in my mind unbidden. Red, clad only in the flimsiest matching red bra and panties. Red, standing in front of the shower performing that impossible woman's maneuver of unfastening her bra. I wish now that I had not averted my eyes then. My physical reaction to these images is not unexpected after such a long dry spell. I need to find a way to take care of this, but my manly pride is holding me back. Looks like I need another shower, a cold one this time.

Stripping down, I turn on the water in the shower as

cold as it will go and step under it. Icy needles of freezing water beat against my skin, raising gooseflesh and shriveling my problem. I stand it as long as I can, and then turn the water on hot so I can lather up. As I dry off with the thick white terry cloth towel, I murmur her name—not Red, but her real name. *Amanda.* She has no idea that I know her real name, and I wonder if she's finally going to tell it to me tonight.

I *AM* GETTING BETTER at this. This is by far the best disguise Red has used, but even she, as good as she is, makes an occasional mistake. Her gait. Her outward appearance bears no resemblance at all to the woman I'm familiar with, but there is no mistaking the way she moves. For me, her walk is a dead giveaway. I spotted her before the show, before she ever sat down at the table in the front row with a man I've never seen before. Despite recognizing her and despite pangs of jealousy, I manage to conceal my emotions during my bit, and my delivery is perfect. The audience loves me.

I don't even take a break. I come directly off the stage into the meet and greet. I'm wracking my brain for a clever way to let her know that I recognized her, so to give myself more time, I circle to the right, making hers among the last tables I visit before the next set starts.

The overhead lights flicker twice, the two-minute warning, as I near her table. As I get closer, I begin to have my doubts. I can't detect a trace of makeup on her, yet her face is seamed and wrinkled, and much fuller. Her dress is very expensive, but the body inside it appears plump and round. Even her shoes look like sensible, old lady shoes. In the end, it's her eyes that give her away. The brown contacts she's wearing can't disguise the pattern of those gold streaks in her irises.

"I really enjoyed your show," she says as we shake hands. She's done a fabulous job of changing her voice, and the twinkle in her eyes tells me she thinks she has me fooled. I have a surprise for her.

Leaning forward as if to kiss her cheek while I still hold her hand in mine, I gently nip her earlobe with my teeth and thrust the tip of my tongue into her ear. The makeup job is awesome, but there's no mistaking the taste of foundation and latex. She's wearing a sophisticated mask that has obviously been fitted by a real pro. To give credit where credit is due, Red manages to keep a straight face.

"Thank you, ma'am. I'm glad you liked it."

I give her a brief smirk and then shake hands with her companion. There's nothing at all familiar about him.

I'M ALREADY STRETCHED out on the easy chair, my feet propped up on the ottoman, when Red enters the suite. I need to figure out how she does that.

"How'd you figure it out?"

"The way that you walk."

That brings a smile to her face, though I don't know whether she's pleased that I paid attention to her teachings or that I've noticed the way she walks.

"We need to talk, Drew."

I watch in fascination as she sits down at the table and leans forward with her open palm under her eyes, popping the contacts out. Dumping them on the table, she reaches up with her free hand, snatches the gray wig off her head, and shakes her head vigorously before running her fingers through her short pixie hairdo. That done, she uses her thumbs and forefingers to grasp the upper edges of the latex mask and peels it downward off her face. Strings of adhesive stretch from her face to the mask, snapping off and curling up as it comes off.

She gets up and walks toward the bathroom, unfastening the buttons down the front of her dress as she goes. There's no hint of the warmth she has displayed in the past; she's cold and businesslike. The door closes behind her, and less than a minute later she comes back out in her denim outfit. Apparently she had used them as padding. The dress she'd been wearing is wadded up in a ball in her hands, and she tosses it on the table in front of me.

She points at the dress and the wig. "There's a trash chute down the hall near the elevators. Sometime before you leave in the morning, drop these in it. I'll take care of the mask and contacts myself." She sits down across from me. "We've decided you are ready for the next phase of your training, Drew, but this phase is going to be a little different. It requires you take a two-week hiatus from the tour and travel to a private, isolated compound for intense and highly specialized training."

Nobody said anything to me before about taking two weeks to go off to some spy school, and I'm fed up with being kept in the dark. If this is all legal and aboveboard, then why do I have to go off to some compound to be trained?

"Don't get me wrong, Red. The money is fantastic, and I'm kind of getting a kick out of all these silly games, but unless I get the answers that note mentioned, I'm done with this."

If she calls my bluff, I have enough cash to get by for however long it takes me to pick up the threads of my career. I'm not really looking forward to going back to the grind . . . but she doesn't know that.

"They're not games, Drew, and by now you should know better than to characterize them that way."

I sense her changing tactics, though nothing shows on her face. She reaches out tentatively and takes my right hand in hers as she gives me a shy smile. I hope I don't ever get into a poker game with this woman.

"The compound is on an island off Puerto Rico, Drew, and there will be no one there but you and me."

Her forefinger is softly stroking the side of my thumb and her actions have the effect on my body she intends, but this time my brain wins the struggle.

"That sounds fantastic, Red, but I've had enough. I want some answers."

"I'm not going to give you answers when you're acting like that. I've given you enough. If you want more, I'll have to check with the higher ups."

She's trying to tell me her special treatment is over. But I'm calling her bluff now.

"Then you'd better check higher up . . . *Amanda*."

That gets her attention.

CHAPTER TWELVE

MIAMI INTERNATIONAL AIRPORT

I'M the only one of the tour group on the flight to Miami. We have a scheduled break for Christmas, and the others chose to go home instead of coming down here like I did. There's nobody back home I particularly want to see. I do my best to stay away from my ex, and I don't have any family left in Detroit, so I don't have any reason to go there. The tour is footing the bill here in Miami, I've got plenty of cash, and sun and sand sound a hell of a lot more fun than ice and snow in Detroit.

The first thing I see as I step off the jetway is a guy in a black chauffeur's suit, hat and all, holding a sign with my name on it. To say that I'm surprised would be an understatement.

I point at the sign in his hand. "That's me."

He gives me a broad smile. "This way sir. You needn't bother with your luggage; the skycap will bring it to the limo."

I'm not comfortable with that, considering that most of my stash is in my suitcase.

"Indulge me."

His smile says he's used to lunatics as he complies with my request. When I give him a hundred-dollar bill and tell him to ditch the sign, it's plain to see that he has added "egomaniac" to the label he has hung on me. There is, however, reason enough to complain about the sign. The luggage carousel at the airport is the most obvious place for a tail to wait for a mark.

THE LIMO IS a shiny black stretch, and my suite in the South Beach hotel is much larger and nicer than I've gotten used to. I tip the bellman and wait for him to leave before inspecting the invisible seals I placed on my luggage before I left the hotel in Kansas City. I'm a lot more thorough in my inspection now, having been fooled by Red at least once. Satisfied that the bags haven't been tampered with, I wander through the suite. To my surprise, there are two bedrooms, a living room, and a full-size dining area, which makes me wonder what sort of revelation Red has planned for me. Right on the heels of that thought, it occurs to me that I'm long overdue for a visit from Duffy. After my conversation with Red, I'm sort of expecting to see him during the break. After all, he's the next one up in the chain, right?

The balcony looks out over the ocean, and of course,

the beach below. The natural scenery is amazing, but the bronzed female bodies in minuscule bathing suits draw my eyes like magnets. I've got some time to myself over the next week or so; maybe it's time for me to abandon my hopeless pursuit of Red and do something about my dry spell. It would at least enable me to think more clearly when I'm dealing with her.

There is a huge pool deck below, dotted with umbrella-covered tables occupied by fetching young lasses in a desperate competition to expose the greatest amount of bare flesh without getting arrested. Waitstaff flit between tables delivering food and drinks, which reminds me that I didn't eat breakfast this morning. My stomach is as hungry as my eyes, and I think it's time to feed both, but not until I shower and change clothes. Judging from the men I've seen since I arrived, I think I need to make a visit to a decent tailor while I'm here. I'm not going to waste any money, but I think I'm going to replace my wardrobe. Even if I go back out on my own, I have changed. Hoodies, jeans, and sneakers work just fine for college crowds, but I've seen a different world than I'm used to up close and personal, and I find myself wanting to fit in.

The walls, floors, and tub in the bathroom are all made of different types of marble, and all the soaps, shampoos, and toiletries have the same scent, jasmine or juniper or something like that. I'm a city boy, not so great with flowers. Wrapped in plastic on the heated towel rack is a pristine white terry cloth robe with a gold hotel monogram embroidered on the left breast.

I'm feeling kingly as I strip off the wrapper and shrug into the robe.

I'm really looking forward to a feast, both visual and gustatory, when a nagging suspicion, or perhaps a premonition, slithers into my consciousness. Tonight will be important. Almost defiantly, I take my dressiest blazer and slacks from my suit bag and lay them out on the bed. Undergarments and a freshly laundered shirt come from the suitcase, and I begin to dress.

Mentally reviewing every step I have taken from the time I got on the plane in Kansas City until I got out of the shower a few minutes ago, I can't think of a single thing I might have missed. Situational awareness has become a watchword for me. I'm virtually certain that I haven't picked up a tail at any point. I checked the tells on my luggage minutely before I opened them. The red leather-bound book is intact and appears to be untouched. I didn't count every single bill, but the wrappers around the stacks of hundreds are still there. I even read the personals section of the *Miami Herald*. No aardvark. Every security protocol Red taught me, I have followed religiously.

Having eliminated my worries about a misstep, I move on to the next logical rung in the ladder: Red. I skip over that step in the progression quickly. I sense no trace of Red's hand in this. Duffy is another matter, as is Jason Keene. Either of them could easily be the higher up Red was referring to in our last conversation. Am I finally going to get some answers? It's about time.

Still a little uneasy, I finish dressing, even going so

far as to put on the necktie Duffy talked me into buying. I'm not sure what's about to happen, but I'm determined not to let anybody put me on the defensive. With a final adjustment to the double Windsor knot on my necktie, I start for the door to the hallway, but I never reach it. The landline in the suite rings.

"Hello?"

"Drew?"

I recognize Jason's voice. "Yeah?" I try, unsuccessfully, to keep the growing belligerence out of my voice.

"Stay. In a very few minutes you're going to have dinner in your suite with a man who *will* make or break your career—both of them. Do you understand?"

I'm pretty sure I know now what a pawn on a chessboard feels like, and it makes me feel small. My belligerence goes up a notch.

"You sound pretty sure of yourself, Jason. What makes you think I even intend to continue with this bullshit game? Maybe I've had enough . . ."

There is a moment of silence on the line, and then I hear Jason's firm, reasoned voice in my ear.

"You and I both know you've come too far to turn back."

The phone line goes dead in my hand, and my blood curdles. I put the handset back in its cradle very slowly and carefully. I've known Jason for years, and thought I knew him well, but this is a side of him I'm not familiar with. I don't like being scared of him. Sinking down into one of the chairs in a state of semi-shock, I try to gather my thoughts without a great deal of success. Up until this moment, only the money has been real. The rest of it—the spook stuff, the prospect of having Red, my future missions—has all been an exciting game. The overt threat and Jason's voice has changed all that. I question my own sanity, because despite the obvious danger, I find myself more eager than ever to participate, even excel, in this dual fantasy life.

Sitting impatiently, drumming my fingers on the tabletop and fidgeting, I wait to hear a knock on the door that indicates the "man"—whoever that is—has arrived to give me the explanations I've demanded. The knock never comes. A minute later, a waiter and a tuxedoed member of hotel management enter the suite rolling a large cart loaded down with an incredibly expensive meal. Tuxedo is carrying a silver champagne bucket filled with chipped ice and a magnum of Dom Pérignon. My eyebrows rise in surprise as Tuxedo sets the bucket on a stand that the waiter has whisked from the bottom level of the food cart and set up on the floor beside the table. Tuxedo, very stiff and prissy, gives me a practiced half bow.

"Champagne compliments of the house, sir. Your guest should be arriving at any moment now."

My *guest*?

Wordlessly, the two set out several dishes and platters with silver dome covers, linen napkins in silver rings, and silver flatware, and then leave. Stunned into immobility for several minutes, I finally reach out and check beneath the silver covers. Some of the food is easily identifiable, like the lobster. Some of it is not, like the gray stuff studded with truffles and surrounded by tiny rounds of toast. The caviar I've seen before, but there's no way in hell I'm putting that crap in my mouth, no matter how expensive it is. Somebody has gone to great expense to impress me.

When my *guest*—a very fit, well-groomed, and impeccably tailored man with manicured hands—arrives, he doesn't bother knocking either. He walks to the table and takes the seat across from me. Although he does not appear much older than me, he has an indefinable air about him that I can only describe as regal. Whoever he is, he's accustomed to being in command of every situation. For some reason, I find that irritating.

"Who the hell are you?" I intend it to come out as a kind of symbolic show of dominance, but even to my own ears, I sound petulant and maybe a little whiny.

"My name is not germane to the matters at hand, Drew." His accent is clipped and precise, almost British, but more likely from somewhere in New England. An envelope appears as if by magic in his hand, a plain white one much thicker than any I've received so far, and he leans forward to set it on the table in front of me. "That's for services rendered so far, and your acceptance of it in no way intimates commitment to further service on your part."

I'm not sure what he's trying to tell me. In my eyes, it's too late to turn back. Red has given me multiple warnings, and Jason all but threatened me during my phone call with him. In any case, he has my full and undivided attention. The envelope is *really* thick.

"We should go ahead and eat while we have a little chat. It would be a shame to waste this food. The chef is an acquaintance, and I can assure you that he makes a splendid *pâté de foie gras*." He lifts the cover off the plate of gray stuff and uses a tiny silver knife to spread a generous dollop of gray paste onto one of the rounds of hard toast. Unwilling to appear uncultured or rude, I mimic his moves and take a nibble of the toast and immediately wish I hadn't. I don't even want to know what he paid for this crap.

Uh oh.

Now I'm getting it. My *guest*. The already nasty aftertaste in my mouth from the foie gras suddenly becomes nastier. I've never been a big fan of champagne, and I suddenly have a craving for an ice-cold beer—a craving as alien to me as the gray crap.

To hell with it. I'm paying for everything anyway, so I'll drink whatever I damned well please. I offer no explanation for my departure from the table. I simply walk over, lift the receiver on the phone, and order a couple of Heinekens from room service. My guest's expression doesn't change, but I'll bet he's filing away a mental note regarding my preference.

"So, what shall we *chat* about?" I try not to sound sarcastic, but not successfully.

"I'll chat, Drew. You listen." He hasn't eaten more than a bite of the foie gras or the caviar, but he wipes his lips carefully with a linen napkin before continuing.

He is smooth and articulate, and he picks at the expensive meal almost delicately as he talks. "For reasons that will become obvious to you in the near future, I will not be revealing the purpose of your employment. It is sufficient for you to know that you are going to be involved in what amounts to industrial espionage. Nothing you will be required to do will be illegal."

We are interrupted by room service delivering my Heinekens, and my guest uses the interruption to open the Dom Pérignon and pour himself a flute of the bubbly stuff. He doesn't speak again until we are once more alone.

"You will be provided an array of credit cards registered in the name of shell corporations located in the Cayman Islands, Lichtenstein, and the Bailiwick of Jersey. An anonymous numbered personal account has been established for you in the Caymans, and that is where future compensation will be wired. The credit cards will cover all of your expenses. You won't be needing your apartment in Detroit. We will treat CTA headquarters as your home of residence for mail, legal documents, and the like."

"Wait just a minute! What do you mean I won't be needing my apartment? It's not like I spend every day of the year on the road." I feel justified in interrupting this pompous ass. I find condescension intolerable, especially from such an arrogant prick as this one.

My interruption hasn't ruffled him in the least. "The agency maintains a large number of corporate residences all over the world. You can pick one and use it as a semi-permanent base, or you might choose to summer in Malibu and winter on the Riviera. Whatever and wherever you desire," he continues.

What I most want to know is what all this training has been for. His answer barely satiates my curiosity.

"Your job will be passing information."

As much as I believe I deserve more details, I know better than to ask this man for more than he's giving me. "No drugs?" I ask suspiciously.

"As I have said, nothing illegal."

"And all I have to do is pass information?"

"There may be more you can do for us in the future. Only time will tell, Drew." He takes a sip from his champagne flute. "One more thing, Drew. That is, if you're in?"

"What's that?"

"Can I take that as confirmation that you wish to continue?"

Is it really possible for me to say no at this point? Jason warned I'm in too deep—maybe it wasn't a threat at all, but a friendly warning not to turn this down. In any case, I'd need to be an idiot not to accept. I nod my head yes.

"Excellent!" He drains the crystal flute in one swallow and stands up, shooting his cuffs and checking the razor-sharp creases of his trousers with his thumbs and forefingers exactly the way Jason had. "Don't give Amanda such a hard time, Drew. She's your immediate supervisor from here on in, and her word is law as far as you're concerned. She really is one of the very best we have."

RED MOVED into the second bedroom of the suite the same day my guest with no name visited. Not that it did me any good. What it has done is put a real crimp in my style. All those gorgeous women in micro-bikinis on South Beach? No such luck. I'd happily immerse myself in my work, but Red hasn't given me another assignment yet, and every time I try to talk to her about it, she says, "Not now."

On the bright side, I will be spending two weeks alone with her, but I don't know exactly where or when yet. That's driving me crazy, the not knowing. I shouldn't complain—the last envelope I received had ten grand inside—but I think I deserve to be treated like an adult instead of a kid who can't keep a secret.

"HEY BUDDY! I don't know what you're doing down there, but keep it up!"

Todd *never* calls me buddy, and it makes me a little nervous that he's doing it now.

"What are you talking about Todd?"

"Drew, the phone's been ringing off the hook. People are calling from all over to book you—a lot of them corporate gigs. You're getting rave reviews in the press, and I'm starting to get calls from some of the trendier radio and television talk shows. And get this! The guys in program development over at Vidxy have sent out some feelers about a special!"

Todd is over the moon about the sudden commercial interest in me, and I am too . . . but I'm also painfully aware of how it coincides with my meeting with the stuffed shirt from CTA.

"Don't schedule anything too soon, Todd. I've still got to finish this tour you know."

"Hey, we have to strike while the iron is hot, dude, but I'm not stupid. This gig is a gold mine, and it's really going to pay off in the long run. I'm sure of that now. The offers are coming in fast and furious, so many of them that I can pick and choose the ones that pay the best. It's really amazing how they're coming in, almost as if somebody set it up on a convenient route for a tour."

I'll just bet they are. How much did he know, if anything, about this little side gig they were going to offer me before we started this odyssey? Did Jason come to him about this? Did Todd get wind of the program and approach Jason about it?

I've never been the suspicious type, but dealing with Red and Duffy during these last few weeks has made me look at everything with a more skeptical eye. I've come to learn that very few of the realities of this business are exactly what they appear to be.

"Gotta jet now. I'm supposed to have drinks with one of the guys from Vidxy, and you don't want me to be late now, do you?" He's gone before I can remind him to be careful about scheduling any gigs too soon.

Vidxy. The most popular reality television network? The very network *America's Funniest Comic* aired on? The one Jason mentioned in his threatening phone call?

Something tells me CTA's behind it. And based on what Red said about me being pulled from this tour? CTA's behind the success of every single person in Vidxy's shows.

WHEN RED WALKS in after wherever she's been, I confront her again. This time I intend to mean it.

"Out of time, Red. Why are you keeping me in the dark about my next training session? Where the hell are we going?" I've made a sincere effort to keep the irritation out of my voice, but I can see from the defensive look on her face that I have screwed up once again. Now she's pissed.

Not that it matters. She may be the boss, but it's high time she learned that I have become a serious student and espionage devotee. "I've been busting my ass to do everything you've asked of me, and even though I haven't gotten everything letter-perfect, you've chosen to keep me in the program. Even Jason and the big boss know that, so why am I still in the dark?" My fists are balled on my hips, and I'm giving her my best fake glare. Just as I'm beginning to believe I've made some headway, I see her lips curl into a small smile.

"Not bad. Not quite good enough, Drew, but it will have to do for now. You just don't muster enough of the 'bad boy' to carry it off." She lays a folder on the table and flips it open. "Sit down, we have some things to talk about." The smile is gone from her lips, and those green eyes bore into mine in deadly earnest.

"First things first. There is a reason I haven't given you my name, but there's no need to go into that now, especially since you've apparently already learned it. I'd give a great deal to know which one of those smarmy bastards told you . . ." She gives me a measuring look, but I'm not biting. I've been on the sharp end of her mysterious ways long enough to know that I won't score points by throwing Jason under the bus.

"My name is Amanda Lewis, and I'm senior trainer for this program. For your general fund of information, there are usually three or four candidates going through the pre-training evaluation. All you've accomplished so far is establishing that you are trainable and that you have the temperament and self-control for the job. During the next phase of your training, you will have my full and undivided attention for two weeks of the most rigorous, intensive instruction you have ever experienced. I'll warn you, an inordinate number of candidates wash out of this phase of the training."

I have questions, but something in her face tells me now is not the time to ask them. She waits, her eyes still locked with mine, presumably to see if I'm stupid enough to interrupt her. I'm not.

My attention is drawn to the open folder on the

table when she plants her forefinger dead center in a section of map.

"Monito Island. That's where we'll be training. It's a barren, uninhabited island fifty miles off the west coast of Puerto Rico. It is inaccessible by sea because it rises straight up out of the water to a height of over two hundred feet. We have maintained a semi-permanent training base there for the last thirty years. The island spans only thirty-six acres, and a large part of it is wooded, but it's big enough to serve our purposes.

"The island itself has been designated an ecological reserve. The Air Force once used it as an aerial bombing range after World War II, and there are still bomb fragments and impact craters there, but you'll need to respect the land and the wildlife.

"Tomorrow you'll travel there by helicopter. You'll be alone for the first two days, a kind of test of your resourcefulness. The chopper will drop you off on the island, but you will take no equipment of any kind with you. All you will be permitted is the clothes on your back—and boots of course. I'm assuming you still have the ones I got for you in Vail?"

"Yeah, I still have them."

"Any resource you find on the island is yours for the using. You are permitted and even encouraged to make yourself as comfortable as you are able. At the end of two days, I will join you, and your training will begin in full. Keep in mind that the comfort of your stay on Monito will depend on how well you utilize the available resources during that first two days."

"Nothing? I can't carry anything with me at all?"

"Only the clothes on your back. No pocketknife, no matches, no magnifying glass you can use to start a fire, nothing. You can only use the resources already available on the island itself."

"Something tells me I'm not gonna like this."

"You're not supposed to like it, Drew. You're supposed to learn from it."

THE FLIGHT from Miami to Isla Verde International Airport, located in Carolina, about three miles from San Juan, Puerto Rico, is a short one. I am met by an unremarkable man dressed in old-fashioned military fatigues with no insignia sewn on them. He doesn't speak to me at all, he just pats me down on the tarmac outside the airplane. Apparently satisfied that I'm in compliance with Red's instructions and that I'm not hiding any machetes or machine guns, he leads me on a fairly long walk across the tarmac to a large steel hangar. The massive doors to the hangar seem to slide open of their own volition. I don't see anyone else present in the hangar.

In the center of the concrete floor sits a highly polished, obviously well-maintained, but still ancient UH-1. The technology is old; the "Huey" was phased out of the U.S. inventory well before I ever enlisted in the National Guard, but it remains one of the most reliable helicopters ever to fly. This one looks like it just came off a showroom floor.

The guy in fatigues, still not talking, motions me toward the chopper, and by means of hand signals indicates we should push it outside the hangar. Easy enough to accomplish since there are small wheels attached to the skids. After a short preflight inspection, the guy climbs into the pilot's seat and points me toward the copilot's seat. In a remarkably short time, we are beating through the air in the direction of Mayaguez, but the chopper doesn't stop there, it just heads out over the open sea.

In less than an hour we're fluttering down onto what looks like a tabletop mesa rising up out of the Caribbean. My pilot doesn't even let the skids touch ground. He simply motions me out of the chopper while he hovers about three feet in the air. Thirty seconds later, I am alone. I see no buildings, no springs, no freshwater of any kind, and the only area that could conceivably protect me from the elements is the stand of scraggly windblown trees occupying a little over half the island.

Shit.

CHAPTER THIRTEEN

ISLA MONITO, PUERTO RICO

I STILL HAVE a knot in my bicep from the typhoid shot they gave me, and I'm sweating in the eighty-degree heat. They weren't joking when they said this place is barren, either. When I saw the trees covering most of the surface area, I was encouraged, but that hope didn't last long.

It only takes a couple of hours to give the place a quick walkover, and I can't help but feel a little put out. There doesn't seem to be any wildlife other than birds and geckos, so I don't feel that I'm in danger. What does concern me is the fact that I haven't found a drop of fresh water, and I've been sweating like a pig. I'm thirsty as hell, and my mouth is dry. I remember the old Spaghetti Western reruns, and from somewhere in the depths of my mind, I recall a cowboy trick of sucking on pebbles to keep from being thirsty. Quite pleased with myself for remembering such an obscure piece of survival information, I squat down and select two small pebbles from the ground in the shade of a small grove of trees and plop them in my mouth.

What the cowboys neglected to mention was that the trick was just that—a trick. All I'm doing is collecting more saliva in my mouth, which is probably going to make me thirstier faster. I spit the pebbles out and rack my brain for any other obscure fact that could help me. The Lone Ranger's pal was a guy named Tonto, which means "fool" in Spanish, and Tonto's nickname for his Ranger pal, *ke-mo sah-bee,* sounds a lot like the Spanish phrase *quien no sabe,* meaning "he who doesn't know." All of a sudden, I lose a lot of faith in what I learned from every western movie I have ever seen. How much more Hollywood bullshit do I have socked away in my head?

I rack my brain, trying to separate what I learned in basic training from what I *thought* I learned from the movies. It's all jumbled up in my head. Thank god it's only two days. I can make two days sitting on my ass in the shade waiting for Red. I find a bare spot under the trees and lean back, planning to get a little nap and rest up from my labors of the morning. It only takes an hour of lying back watching the gulls fly overhead before I am bored out of my skull . . . and thirsty as hell. The heat isn't so bad, but the humidity is ridiculous, and the sweat isn't evaporating from my skin, making me feel hotter. It's dry as hell on this rock, but I'm soaking wet anyway. *It's only two days, Drew, you can do this. It's all in your head.*

I know this isn't the first time this place has been used to train an operative, and that means I should have seen some sign of human habitation when I explored earlier. With a muttered curse, I get up off my ass and glance around. Nothing.

Come on, Drew, use your head. You're no Boy Scout, but you have to remember something, anything from your Guard training. The south end of this pitiful rock is the lowest. There's a thicker growth of trees along a depression that turns into a fissure near the sheer cliff that drops off into the Caribbean. If there's any place here more human-friendly, I haven't seen it. I must not be looking hard enough.

At the end of the first day, I still haven't found any obvious sign, but there is subtle evidence of activity along the fissure. The crack is deep, and if I weren't so worn out, I might consider negotiating it to get down closer to the ocean. As it is, I think I'll crash under these trees for the night. I wish that pebble trick worked, but I can still taste that limestone in my dry mouth, so it's probably better this way. Maybe I'll try the stem of one of these sawgrass plants.

I'M UP AT DAYBREAK, and my back aches from sleeping on the ground . . . if you can call what I did last night sleeping. My mouth is dry as hell and it tastes like some baby wild thing used it as a potty. The sawgrass was moist but very bitter, and it didn't help much. I'll concentrate on making myself a little more comfortable tonight, maybe break off some branches and spread them under the trees. The temperature was okay, and the bugs didn't bother me too much last night.

I need to relieve myself, so I walk well away from my sleeping area and let it rip. Wonder how I'll deal with that after Red gets here. Thinking of me and her alone on this rock for a couple of weeks sends my imagination soaring to places it shouldn't go for a few minutes. I close my eyes and get a vivid image of how she looked when she hopped out of my bed in Denver and held that wicked-looking blade against my throat. I can see every soft curve of her body in that lacy red bra and matching panties. I remember the way she felt against me in her barn outside Vail, her breasts pressed against me as she straddled me and kissed me.

I have to stop this thought process. Knowing her, she'll show up tomorrow and do her level best to try to kill me. She warned me this was going to be tough.

The sun is rising and the light casts shadows that I didn't see yesterday. The subtle traces along the fissure I wasn't sure of before are a little more obvious now. I follow them along the deep crack about halfway down the length of the fissure and notice a faint dip along the edge. Lying down on my belly, I lean out as far as I dare over the chasm and look down. About twelve feet down there is a narrow ledge leading toward the sea end of the fissure. As near as I can tell it comes to an end about sixty feet above the water. I can't see any obvious handholds, and I'm not about to drop down to the ledge without knowing if I can get back out again.

Pushing up to my hands and knees, I back away from the edge and then stand up. If people are getting down to that ledge, there has to be an anchor point for a rope or a ladder somewhere nearby, so I walk over to the tree line and check out the backs of the tree trunks that look stout enough to hold a man. Sure enough, there's a tree with some of the bark rubbed off toward the bottom of the trunk about ten paces back from the fissure. Mystery solved, and I now know that the ledge figures in with the training somehow. I wonder if there's a rope stashed somewhere up here . . .

Three hours of fruitless searching later, I'm parched. It's getting hot, and I'm no closer to solving the conundrum of the ledge. *Tell me one more time why you agreed to this lunacy, Drew? Oh yeah, I remember. Fame, fortune, and of course, getting into Red's panties. Fat chance! Get your head out of your butt, and make yourself as comfortable as possible for the night. She'll be here tomorrow, and she really doesn't want to kill you. There's money in this for her, so she won't let you die, even if she roughs you up some during the training.*

I go about gathering limbs, brush, and anything else I can find to make a bed under the trees.

MY MAKESHIFT BED is a little less uncomfortable than the bare ground, and when I open my eyes the sun is a little higher in the sky than it had been yesterday when I got up. My tongue feels like sandpaper, and again a foul taste makes me think I'm serving as a litter box.

I'm not sure where it's coming from at first. There's a sound like a sheet of plastic blowing in the wind nearby, but I know better. There isn't an inch of this rock I haven't seen by now, and I haven't seen any manmade materials at all yet. I don't know what makes me look up—maybe the piercing cry of the seabirds— but there she is. Red. Gliding through the air on one of those light green ram air parachutes like I've seen on television. The fluttering sound is coming from the parachute as she steers it into the wind. I watch, riveted, as she brings it to a soft landing just feet away from me.

"I didn't hear the plane."

"Small plane, fifteen thousand feet. You wouldn't be able to hear it at that altitude. That's why we jump from that high."

"We?"

"You won't be learning to jump this trip. That will come later. *If* you get through this phase, Drew." She gives me an appraising look. "I'm not convinced yet that you can."

I bridle a little at that. My male ego has been ruffled, but Red doesn't notice it. She's bent over and busily wadding up her chute. I should be concentrating on what she's gonna do with that parachute—it would make a hell of a tent—but instead I'm appreciating the curve of her rump where those camouflage pant stretch tight. I don't get to look long.

"All right, Drew, I guess you didn't find it." She lays the wadded-up chute down, unbuckles the chest strap, and steps out of the harness.

"Find what?"

Exasperated sigh. "The cache, Drew. The reason we sent you out here with nothing was to challenge you to use your wits and push your personal envelope. Stretch your comfort zone. Field work is different. You not only need survival skills, you need to *think*. To learn to take advantage of any available assets."

"There's nothing available on this rock, Red, I've been over every inch of it." My own exasperation is showing, and she hasn't been here five minutes yet.

"Oh really?" Her voice is dripping sarcasm. I watch as she walks over to the edge of the fissure and then turns to give me a sour look. "Did you look here?"

"Yeah, and I found where the bark is scraped off that tree for an anchor point, but there's no rope . . ."

I get a disgusted look, and then she drops down onto her belly and leans so far over the chasm that I'm scared she's going to fall. She has one hand on the lip and the other hand stretched down into the fissure. In about ten seconds she comes up with a waterproof canvas bag covered in limestone dust and gull shit.

"The rope is right here. All you had to do was make an effort to go down into the fissure and you would have seen it. For Pete's sake, Drew, I told you we use this place for training, and anybody with half a brain could have spotted the signs of human passage. Even you did. Why didn't you try to go over the edge?"

I'm uncomfortable now. I don't want her to know I was afraid of falling into the fissure. For some reason I'd rather her think I'm dumb instead of afraid. I shrug.

"I didn't think of it. I was too focused on where you might have hidden the rope." I don't know if she bit, but she snatches the rope out of the bag and tosses it to me. It's a nylon military rappel rope, just like I'd used in basic training, coiled and wrapped the same way.

Hands on her hips, she glares at me. "Can you at least tie a bowline?"

This I can handle. I walk over to the tree and mentally review the process for tying a bowline, performing each step to make the knot. "Up through the rabbit hole, round the big tree; down through the rabbit hole, and off goes he." I add an extra loop with the working end of the rope when I form the "rabbit hole," making a double bowline that won't slip. Tugging on the running end of the rope to tighten it, I look up at Red with a great deal of satisfaction. Let her find fault with that!

"What are you waiting for, Drew? An invitation?"

She's not even going to show me. She expects me to body rappel over the lip of the chasm and find whatever is concealed there myself. I hate body rappelling, always did. It left me with rope burns on my back when I did it in basic training, and I'm allergic to pain, but I'm not about to back down in front of Red. I still don't know if she's talked to Ed and Ethel, and I don't want to piss her off in the least. I feel like I'm on very shaky ground right now, and I have developed a real interest in this program. It's not just the money and my career anymore. I really want to learn to be the best at this. I have a long way to go, and I know it.

I grit my teeth and back up to the edge of the fissure. The first step off is the worst. If I slip here or allow too much slack in the rope, I'm going to smack into the limestone wall face first, and maybe just let go and fall into the cleft to my death. My stomach lurches as I lean back, and suddenly I am in the correct L position, my feet on the wall, my spine upright, and I am looking at the hollowed-out spot where the rope bag was concealed. It's an overhang where no one who didn't know exactly where it was located could have spotted it from a different angle.

The ledge is a good eight feet below me still, and it looks narrow as hell. Easing my grip on the rope wrapped across my back, around my waist, and clenched tightly to my chest, I lower myself the eight feet a little at a time, maintaining foot contact with the wall face. With my feet firmly planted on the ledge, I do not relinquish my death grip on the rope. I'm not confident about the strength of this ledge, and I know I have to get back out of here, too.

The wall face is pocked with openings, but I can't see any indication of which one might contain Red's cache.

"Which one is it?"

"You're going to have to earn your money this time, Drew. Ed's not here to help you now."

Shit. She knows! Has she passed that information up the chain? If she had, I don't think I would be here now. For some reason she gave me a pass on that one, and I have no idea why. I've got a lot riding on these two weeks . . .

I'm not trusting my weight to this ledge. Firming up my grip on the rope with both hands, I flex my knees and push off from the wall face, hopping to the right a few feet so I can see into the next opening. No joy. It takes two more hops before I find the cache.

"Got it!" I yell out in exultation.

"Good for you." That sounded like sarcasm to me, but in my joy, I let it slide. There are two army duffel bags inside the pocket cave, and a waterproof bag next to them. I step inside the cave and wrap the running end of the rappel rope around my waist. Can't afford to lose that. I wasn't sure the ledge would hold my own weight when I came down, so I sure as hell won't trust it to hold my weight and the weight of a heavy duffel bag on the way back up.

When I open the waterproof bag, my heart nearly explodes. I don't know which makes me happier, the rope grabs or the three twenty-ounce bottles of water, but I know which one I'm using first. I'm almost panting as I twist the cap off the first bottle and drain it without stopping to breathe. I catch my breath as I snatch the second bottle and down that one, too. I sit down and stare at the third bottle for a minute. Should

I save it for Red? Doesn't take me long to come to a conclusion. Screw it. She just got here, and I've been dry for two days. I open the bottle and lean back against the cave wall, sipping and thinking.

The rope grabs are a godsend. With these two devices I can climb out of here easily. None of that Batman and Robin shit for me! Two heavy duffel bags will pose a problem, though. I can only carry one at a time, and two bags means I will have to make two separate ascents. Unless . . .

This decision doesn't take long either. These ropes have a tensile strength of about twenty-five hundred pounds—way more than the combined weight of me and these two duffel bags. I tie the bags to the end of the rappel rope (I'm so tickled I almost forget to slip on the rope grabs before tying the duffels on) and let them hang while I climb the rope to the top of the wall. Red and I lift them up together

"Took you long enough."

I feel no guilt at all about drinking that third bottle of water.

Twelfth Day On Isla Monita

Every bone in my body aches, and I haven't slept in days, but I survived. I stink, I haven't shaved, and it is entirely possible that I fractured my wrist yesterday. Red switched gears in the middle of a lesson on surveillance techniques and started a spontaneous review of hand-to-hand combat by executing an over-the-shoulder throw and trying to pin me by twisting my wrist and placing her boot in the small of my back. I bowed up, elbowed her in the pelvic area (very satisfying), and twisted away, falling and landing on my wrist. I thought I heard the bones crack, but it might have been my imagination. She says it isn't broken, but it's badly swollen and discolored today. I can barely use it, and Red has had to open all the cans of food we are feasting on. Apparently, we are taking a break.

The chopper came back and dropped supplies off after we finished up what little was stashed in the duffel bags. The first few days we lived off old surplus C-rations packed in the fifties and sixties (yuck). We've been eating pretty good since the chopper resupplied us, but they only left us enough water to drink, nothing to wash with. Both of us are groaty as hell, and I'm fantasizing more about a hot soak than I am about a decent meal.

Something has been bothering me since Red got here, but she has only mentioned it once. This is the first real break we've taken since her arrival, so I set down the can of peach slices I'm eating and clear my throat to get her attention. She glances up from the can of fruit cocktail she is picking at, a vacant look on her face.

"If Ed and Ethel told you how I screwed up, why didn't you go ahead and shitcan me?"

She takes a long time before she answers me, quickly finishing her fruit cocktail, crushing the empty can, and tucking it into our garbage bag. "I really don't know, Drew." She gives me a look I can't interpret. "I should have booted you out of the program. Everything I've learned over the last few years is screaming 'oh hell no,' but my gut is telling me that you could be one of the best I've ever trained." She looks like she wants to say more, but I can see the effort she is putting into shutting her mouth . . . and that bothers me.

"Come on, Amanda, let's have the rest of it."

She frowns at that, and it is several minutes before she answers me. I lean back against a tree trunk and stare up at the gulls soaring high above us while I wait. I used to think those birds were graceful, but since I've been on Isla Monito, I've noticed the way their bodies twitch and shift to keep facing into the wind currents. They expend a lot of energy even when their wings aren't flapping, and they always seem sort of pissed off when they cry out.

"I worried at first that it was because I am more than a little attracted to you."

That makes me jerk upright, but she quickly puts both hands out in a pushing away motion.

"That's not why you're here, Drew, and I have no intention of letting my physical reaction to you get in the way of our business relationship. Get that through your head right now."

That's disappointing, but I somehow manage to refrain from making a smart-ass remark—something I usually can't control.

"There's an indefinable something about you that tells me you're going to be able to handle this job . . . if

I can find a way to keep you focused on the details." She cocks her head to one side and gives me a speculative look. "I just hope I can figure out how to do that before you get yourself killed."

That sends a chill racing up my spine. "Killed? As in *dead*?"

She takes me seriously and nods.

"The businesses we are going to be getting information on tend to go to excesses in protecting that information."

I gulp audibly and ask a question I'm not really sure I want the answer to. "Have any of the operatives you've trained been killed?"

"None of the ones *I've* trained have died, but I'm not the only trainer, and you aren't the only operative in training right now."

That doesn't exactly answer my question, but opens up a whole new world of doubts and questions. Stunned, I get up and walk toward the other end of the island to stare out over the Atlantic while I think over what she just told me.

CHAPTER FOURTEEN

CINCINNATI, OHIO

THE WEATHER here is a hell of a lot different from Isla Monito, and the clothes I bought in Miami when I got back from the training camp aren't suitable for the nasty weather in Cincinnati. What was I thinking?

You were thinking you looked pretty buff after two weeks of hell, and you were reliving reruns of Miami Vice. Sonny Crockett you definitely are not. Unconstructed blazers, shiny fabric jackets, lighter colors, and Italian loafers worn without socks still work in Miami these days, but anywhere else in the world, I'll look like I just walked out of a time warp. I've got to use one of these "shell corporation" credit cards Duffy slipped me at the airport and get some real clothes.

That conversation with Red on the island has changed me. When I look at myself in the mirror now, I see a stranger. I look tougher, more buff, and I have a bitchin' tan . . . but I wonder how my audiences will react to my new look. I'd like to say I don't feel any different, but that would be a lie. I do feel different, more confident. It even shows in the way I carry myself. I need to think about this. One of the lessons Red has drummed into my head all along has been about the necessity of my being innocuous, inconspicuous, just an ordinary guy. For the first time I wonder how I'm going to maintain that image if the agency makes me as famous as they said they would. My thoughts on wardrobe take an unexpected turn. I don't need to adopt the Bond look. I need to adopt the Joe Ordinary look. Well dressed, but conservative . . . but I'm still going to avoid ties like the plague. I have some shopping to do.

On the way out of my suite, I spot the copy of *The Cincinnati Enquirer* that room service left with my breakfast this morning. *Damn it! Haven't you learned anything, Drew?*

I check the personals section, and there they are. "Aardvark" and "bastille" in the first ad. The hell of it is, there is nothing there telling me who, when, where, or how I will be contacted this time. I'm going to have to be ready for anything. There's nothing to do but go about my business. The tour group won't be here for three more days, and I thought Red was cutting me a break, giving me a few days off after the grueling two-week stint on Monito. So much for that happy thought.

∽

I SPENT all day yesterday waiting to be contacted, and I was jumpy as hell—really on edge the whole time I was shopping for my conservative clothing. I guess it's a good thing no one made contact. I was so wired I probably would have muffed it. Today I'm going to chill out, relax, and go about enjoying my day while remaining on the alert for anything that comes up. Stay frosty. The first thing I'm going to do is get something for breakfast. I'm usually health conscious about what I eat, but I've been dreaming about a gluttonous, cholesterol-laden breakfast celebration for days now, and I'm going to indulge myself.

I have good intentions, but one look at the new blazer, button down shirt, and slacks hanging in my closet changes my plans. I can recreate my image later. For now, I'm gonna be comfortable. My old hoodie and jeans come out of my luggage, and I slip my feet into the comfortable athletic shoes I've worn for years.

As I close the door to my suite behind me and place the tiny swatch of clear tape at the top left of my door, I can almost taste the mushroom and cheese omelet I'm going to order the minute I get downstairs. I can feel the crispy texture of bacon on my tongue, and my mouth is watering. Stuffing my key card into the pocket of my hoodie, I speed walk toward the elevator.

The aroma of fine dark roast Columbian coffee welcomes me as soon as the elevator door opens on the ground floor, and in my haste to get to the restaurant I almost run over a slight balding man waiting patiently for the door to open. There are other people waiting to get on, but I'm impatient, and besides, they can't get on till I get off, can they?

I try to go to the balding guy's right, but we get our signals crossed and we both move in the same direction, me trying to get around him and him trying to get out of my way. We tangle up for an awkward second, and then I manage to escape. The guy doesn't even say excuse me. Nobody has manners anymore. His lack of common courtesy doesn't even slow me down. I'm hungry as hell, and the smells coming from the restaurant in the atrium are driving me wild.

THE OMELET IS light and fluffy, covering half my plate, and the combination of cheese and mushrooms is delicious. The golden-brown home fries are crunchy on the outside and tender on the inside. The bacon is utterly crisp and complements the omelet perfectly. The coffee is to die for, and I am stuffed to the gills, but I'm eyeing the billowy cinnamon roll on the plate of a nondescript woman sitting at the next table, and I can smell it from here. My stomach is groaning 'no', but my tongue is telling it to shut up. The intelligent thing to do is compromise. I order a cinnamon roll to go and take it with me in a foam container as I head back to my suite.

There is no line at the elevators, so I have the stainless steel cubicle all to myself. Mind-numbingly bland Muzak assaults my ears as I push the button for my floor, and the savory aroma of the cinnamon roll is doing a number on my head. I wish these things were faster.

The elevator comes to a halt, the doors open, and I am practically running down the hall—either from the Muzak or in my haste to start a pot of coffee and devour this tantalizing sweet roll, I'm not sure which.

In front of my door, I eagerly dip into the pocket of my hoodie for my key card. My hands touch something that shouldn't be there, and I freeze. I know where it came from without thinking. That damned bald guy! He did a bump pass, and I didn't even notice. Some spook I'm turning out to be.

It's On

It's been almost twelve hours since I got the shock of my life. The cipher key was innocuous enough, just like the ones I've been using all along. I found it (after the most thorough search ever) under the insole of one of the very expensive Italian loafers I have decided not to wear anymore. The message, four Post-its printed front and back, is the longest one I've ever had to decrypt. It's also the reason my blood is running like ice through my veins right now.

My eyes are glued to the first line of the decryption.

Start earning your keep. Real world mission.

What kind of insanity is this? No way in hell I'm ready for a real-world mission!

I try to get my heart to stop pounding, but when I

reread the message, I swear my blood pressure skyrockets. I read it again in disbelief, and then I decrypt it again in case I made a mistake the first time. My whole body shifts into panic mode. Cinnamon roll and coffee forgotten, I race to the bathroom and hug the commode while I puke up that delicious breakfast. It doesn't taste nearly as good coming up as it did going down.

Stripping off my clothes, I climb into the shower and turn on the cold water full blast. I have to shock myself out of this panic. I'm in way too deep to back out now. I've taken their money. In my head I can hear the voices of Red, Jason, and Duffy warning me about "consequences."

THE CONCIERGE TELLS me the quickest way to get to the Bell Connector, Cincinnati's streetcar system, is to take an Uber to the Cincinnati Cyclones Station in the Banks, the business section of town near the river. My instructions from the cipher say to ride the tram from the river to Findlay Market in Over-the-Rhine. Findlay Market has been open continuously since before the Civil War, and I've been there before, but this is my first time on the Bell Connector. The Market is a fascinating place, and I love to visit there, but today I'm supposed to go to a street vendor—of Mexican food no less—and ask for a kosher hot dog. There can't be that many pink, two-wheeled carts with a matching canopy and the words "Abdul's Tacos" painted in italics on the side, so I'm not worried about spotting him when I get there. What I'm worried about is the hulking beast sitting three seats back from me on the tram car.

He got on at the first stop we made after leaving the station, and as he walked down the aisle past me, he was staring at me hard enough to make me start sweating bullets. He hasn't gotten off at any of the numerous stops since. What the hell? Have I picked up a tail? Already?

My palms are sweaty when I get off at the Findlay Market stop, but I manage to stay calm as I walk over to one of the old-fashioned streetlamp posts by the stop and lean against it. When the hulk doesn't get off the tram, I heave an audible sigh of relief and stroll on down the street in search of that cart.

I FIND the pink vendor's cart not far from the safety of my lamp post. It's not just pink, it is hot pink, and the vendor doesn't look like any Abdul I've ever seen. He's short and broad, with an overgenerous nose and a mane of kinky black hair that hangs down to his belt in back. He's wearing a lime green t-shirt depicting an angry mouse extending his middle finger at a diving hawk with the legend "Last Great Act of Defiance" printed around it in block letters. The rest of his ensemble comprises dirty athletic shoes and a pair of skinny jeans at least one size too small for him. There are only three people in line ahead of me, but standing here waiting for him to serve them makes me nervous as hell. After a lifetime of Abdul's patter as he makes tacos, I reach the head of the line.

"What'll ya have?"

"I'd like a kosher dog." He gives me a blank look for a few heart-stopping seconds and then his face lights up. I can literally see the lights come on behind those glassy eyes.

"Dude! Was expectin' you earlier. Shoulda known it was you though, cuz you look nervous as hell."

His indiscretion makes me uneasy, and I turn around to see if anyone else heard him, but there's no one else in line, and no one near enough to us to hear.

"Jeez, Abdul, could you keep it down?"

He laughs out loud. "Oh wow! They sent me a cherry this time!" He leans forward conspiratorially and beckons me closer. "People only get suspicious when you do something an' look like you're sneakin'. Din't they teach you that?"

Not in so many words, but Red *did* tell me many times that I have to blend in, look like part of the crowd. When she was being formal, she referred to the technique as situational camouflage. *Look like you know what you're doing, Drew—like you belong. Acting hinky is a dead giveaway, and somebody will stop you or remember you every time you do that.* I pull myself together.

"So, what do we do now, Abdul?"

"I fix you this taco real slow like, and I tell you what your mission really is," he says, reaching for a soft flour tortilla and slapping it on the grill in the cart. "An' by the way, the name is Myron, not Abdul. Want some nachos with this? I got the best nachos around."

The whole scenario is unreal. I'm covered in nervous sweat, and Myron is casually chattering away, giving me my first real assignment while spreading refried beans and taco meat on a tortilla.

"The car is a blue Ford Escort, an old one. Parked on the second level of the underground parking deck in Washington Park. It's got a long-term parking sticker on the windshield, so ya won't have ta pay on the way out, just pull up to the scanners an' wait for the bar to raise."

"Car?"

Myron shakes his head in disgust. "I can't give you your instructions if you're runnin' your mouth. Pick your head up an' watch for anybody getting' close while I finish this, would ya?" He reaches into a stainless bowl and grabs a handful of shredded lettuce and some diced tomatoes.

"The guards only walk the long-term floor at the beginnin' an' end of their shifts. The info ya need is in a thumb drive about yea," he lifts a hand and indicates the size with his thumb and forefinger, "big, but I don't know where it's stashed inside the car. There's supposed to be a spare key up under the left rear fender in a magnetic box—"

"Supposed to be?"

"Hey, I'm just passin' the information to ya like I was told to, the way it was told to me." He tosses a handful of tortilla chips in a small paper tray and drips a ladleful of nacho cheese on them. "Ya want jalapeños on this? They're not too hot, but everybody seems to like 'em just fine."

I stare at him incredulously. He's talking about food I don't even want at the same time as he's telling me I have to break into a car. He puts them on anyway and puts the nachos and the taco up on the counter and slides them toward me.

"That'll be eight bucks."

Flustered, I reach into my pocket, pull out a fifty, and fork it over.

"C'mon, ain't ya got nothin' smaller?"

"Just keep the change. How am I supposed to search the car without being noticed?"

He gives me a surprised look. "Ya gotta take the car someplace else, dude. Can't do it in the parkin' garage. They *do* got cameras in there ya know." He shakes his head ruefully. "Boy, you really *are* a cherry, aren't you?" Myron starts hurriedly closing down the mobile stand.

I stand there staring at him with my mouth open, taco in one hand and nachos in the other. He starts to push the cart away.

"But . . . wait . . ."

"I been talkin' to you too long. I gotta jet." He glances around, looking worried now, and that sends my panic meter into overdrive. "Make sure ya wait until dark, dude. The guards change shift at five."

"Where can I take the car around here?"

"Try the stadium parkin' lot down by the river," he

calls back over his shoulder. He shunts the cart to the side of the street and begins to walk rapidly into the crowd on the sidewalk. He's out of sight before I can say another word, and I'm standing in the middle of the street holding food I have no desire to eat.

What the hell? Nobody said anything about stealing a car. They specifically told me that I wouldn't have to do anything technically illegal.

I wasn't hungry when I got here, and I'm sure as hell not hungry now. I dump everything in a trash can on my way back to my tram stop. I'm watching nervously to see if I've picked up a tail. What if Myron was being watched? He's plainly been doing this for some time, how would I know? Everything has suddenly gotten very real, and I'm very unsure of myself. I dump the food into the trash can and wipe my hands off nervously.

You really want to go back to scraping for rent every month, Drew? Busting your ass for gigs, staying in lousy little cheap motels and eating fast food three times a day . . . when you can afford it? You want to walk away from nice gigs, nice clothes, a house in Malibu, maybe an HBO special or two? You going to give all that up? All that and Red too?

Screw that. I've got a car to steal.

IT ONLY TAKES five minute or so to walk down Elder Street and take a left on Elm down to Washington Park, but after glancing at my watch, I decide to stroll along slowly. I've time to kill before dark, and I want to get a good look at the parking garage before I just walk right in. I also want to make certain I haven't picked up a tail after talking to Myron. I don't have the confidence in him that the people above me in the chain seem to.

After several blocks I catch a glimpse of a guy who seems to be watching me as I walk, and I step into one of the clear plastic trolley stops and take a seat on the bench. It's cold, and there's nobody else sitting here. Traffic on the street is light, and I can see from the posted schedule that the Bell Connector isn't due for a while yet. This gives me the perfect opportunity to check out the guy I spotted a few minutes back.

He walks past me slowly, studiously avoiding eye contact, and that makes me even more suspicious of him. Though not as big as the hulk from the Bell Connector, he's still an intimidating specimen. Forty or so, very fit, a hard face, all angles and planes. Dressed in jeans and an old army field jacket, his sandy blond hair cut short, he carries himself with what I can only describe as a military bearing. He doesn't look at me, but it's easy to tell he is very much aware of me. He looks tough. Scary tough.

I'm not sure he's a tail—after all, the hulk fooled me —but my gut tells me he is. Instead of paralyzing fear, I get an unexpected adrenaline rush. This is not training, this is the real thing. This is where I find out if I have what it takes to be a real operative, and I'm eager to prove myself. I'm scared shitless and exultant at the same time.

The maybe-tail walks on past the trolley stop like he hasn't got a care in the world and disappears down the street. If I'm right about him, he's going to duck inside a storefront or slip into one of the buildings undergoing renovations, and there are a lot of them along Elm Street. Over-the-Rhine is still a developing area, with lots of restaurants and hip new clubs opening every day.

I still have an hour and a half before nightfall, so I give my maybe-tail fifteen minutes or so before I get up and start walking toward Washington Park. I don't see him as I stroll, and my confidence begins to build. I write off my concerns to newbie jitters over my first real assignment. I can't be *too* careful—just because I'm a little paranoid doesn't mean there's nobody out to get me.

There's a sign at the street entrance to the Washington Park garage that says the underground deck is full. It's after five, so I decide to do a little bit of subtle reconnaissance. I want to know exactly where that Escort is, and I need to know the quickest way out of the garage from its location.

IT'S WELL after dark when I locate the Escort, but I've wandered around enough to know how to get out of this hole. No sense waiting around any longer than I have to. It's now or never.

Squatting down beside the left rear fender, I feel around in the wheel well for the little magnetic box the key is supposed to be in, and my heart starts pounding harder when my fingers close on it. I tug on it and the little metal box falls into my palm. My hands are shaking in anticipation as I slide the cover back off the box. There's no key inside, and I feel a jolt in my chest as my hammering heart skips mid-beat. Shit!

I force my heartbeat to slow down, determined not to give up. It's an old car, maybe I can figure out a way to hot wire it. I know it can be done. Even though I'm no great shakes as a mechanic, I've managed to keep my old beater of a car running all these years. I see guys on television do it all the time. Then again, I thought I could quench thirst with rocks.

I'm screwed.

Standing up, I move the two steps to the driver's side door and reach for the handle. Maybe, it won't be locked . . . but it is. I lean over and peer inside at the ignition, and my heart starts racing again. All I have to do is figure out how to get in the damned car! Hoping against hope, I try to insert my fingers through the window gasket and the glass, but I can't budge it.

I hear the footsteps too late. Even as I try to turn around, I feel two strong hands grasping my wrists with a grip like an iron vice. I struggle to see my attacker, but I can't manage to twist around before I'm slammed down onto the hood of the car.

"Boo." The voice is harsh and guttural, and it scares the hell out of me. I'm twisted around until my back is stretched across the hood, the iron hands clutching at the front of my new shirt. Oh, shit! It's my maybe-tail!

CHAPTER FIFTEEN

ALL IN

I DON'T REMEMBER one iota of Red's training about holds. If I'm being honest, I didn't *want* to learn how to escape her grasp. I have the opposite problem now. If I can't get free, I'm dead.

I need a weapon, and I need to find one without him seeing me look. That leaves me with few options, but instantly I know what to do.

With my right hand I grasp his left wrist, acting like I'm trying to break his hold, and with my left, I yank at a windshield wiper with all my might and slash his face with it.

It works. He lets go, pressing a hand against his face. When his palm comes away, I don't see any blood. I hold the windshield wiper out like it's actually usable as a weapon, even though I know he could smash it in half at a thought. But I've got nothing else, and I'm sure as hell not going to lose my dignity, too. Hell, maybe I already have. Look at me. Fending off a giant with a bit of plastic.

"Drew."

"Back off," I say.

He smirks and reaches into a pocket. My insides turn to ice. Everything I learned from Red rushes into me. I'm supposed to bluff and make him think I have a weapon that could kill him. Except that's not possible when I am holding a windshield wiper like it's Excalibur. I've already shown all my cards.

The knife he pulls out doesn't look like something that will kill me quickly and I groan. I'm not good with pain, and now I'm wondering why he's brought a knife to what could have been a gun fight. If he knew he had to stop me, then why didn't he bring a gun? He has to be one of the people Red said would stop CTA at any cost. That means he should have resources and access to spear gear that I don't. Revolvers. Silencers.

Before I can work out his plan, the knife clatters to my feet. I look down at it in disbelief, then back at him, then at the wiper blade in my hands. I'd much prefer the actual blade, and I quickly drop the plastic to pick up the knife.

He laughs. "You look good, Drew. A bit deer-in-the-headlights, but good."

Maybe this means he does have a gun. Now I'm the one who brought a knife to a gun fight.

"Relax, Drew. I'm not here to kill you. I'm here to be killed."

I can feel the color drain from my face. "What?"

"Amanda wants you on real world missions. You need to be able to react. Think on your feet. I'm sure you've been told this quite a few times by now."

"CTA sent you? I thought—"

"That I was really out to get you? Nah." He smiles again and I'm suddenly aware that I still have the knife pointed at his chest. I get out of my horse stance and lower my arm, but not all the way. This could still be a trick.

"Look, I don't know what you're talking about. What do you say we go our separate ways?" What else am I supposed to say? I've gone from a wiper blade to a knife, but somehow I still feel completely unprepared for this fight. Even if I get everything Red taught me right, if he has a gun, and I flub the disarm, there is nothing I can do.

The man just chuckles at me again. "I'm not going anywhere, Drew. CTA did send me, and this is your final test. If you don't kill me, you fail."

He can't be serious. Why would he agree to that? The only way I would ever agree to something like that is if I knew I could win.

"So, what? I'm just supposed to run at you and stab you in the neck? That can't be what's supposed to happen here."

"What's supposed to happen is you're supposed to show you're all in."

"I'm not running at you. You'll shoot me."

"I don't have a gun, Drew."

"Prove it."

I don't expect him to do what he does next. In a minute, he's stripped off every layer of clothing except his boxers, and even those he makes a show of patting to his thighs so I can see he isn't hiding anything. He spins in a full circle and when he faces me again, he folds his arms.

"Good enough for you?" he asks.

I'm floored. "Why would you agree to do this unless you knew you'd live?"

"Ah, Drew. You still don't get it. But you'll learn. There's a lot that money can buy in this field."

"What good is money to you if you're dead?"

"You're not a family man, are you, Drew?"

I shake my head.

"Then you wouldn't understand. Are you going to kill me or what?"

I realize my knuckles have turned white from how hard I'm clutching the knife, so I loosen my grip a bit. I don't know what I'm supposed to do. All I know is that I'm not supposed to be doing anything illegal. If CTA is testing me, that means I'm not supposed to kill him. The right answer has to be walking away.

I start backing away from him. He doesn't budge but he does smile again. "Drew. You don't get out of this. Nobody does."

I don't know if he means this test or CTA. I don't know if I care. As quick as I can, I turn and run. I know I shouldn't look back, but I do, and he's gone. That's when I make the mistake. I stop moving. I'm an idiot, but I don't know where he went, and I'm not about to get snuck up on. I get back into horse stance and watch all around for him to approach. Then out of the corner of my eye, I see the movement. Except it's not a human moving.

It's a car.

"Oh, shit!"

It's too late to run. I dive out of the way onto my stomach, holding onto the knife as tight as I can. Before I can roll over, he's yanking my shirt again and turning me over himself.

"I told you. You can't get out of this."

"I'm not supposed to kill anyone. I'm not supposed to do anything illegal." I'm trying not to sound petulant, but it's impossible at this point.

"It's not illegal if it's self-defense," he says. Then his hands circle my throat.

I panic. I drop the knife and claw at his wrists. He's too strong. I buck my hips, and my brain even now thinks of Red keeping me in this exact position during one of our training sessions in Vail.

"I'm going to kill you if you don't get me off, Drew."
"Do I look like I care?"
She smacks me upside the head and regrips my throat.
"You're dead in ten seconds if you don't do something."
What was I supposed to do? Headbutt her? I reached out my hands which had been gripping her writs, slipped them under her arms, and tickled her armpits.
"Drew!" she yelled as she let go.
"What?"

*I know I saw her smile, but she hid it, and then chastised
me for an hour. "You're never going to make it if you
can't make difficult decisions. If you can't—"
"Think on my feet. I know."
"No. For once, this isn't about thinking on your feet. It's
about doing something that Drew wouldn't do. It's
about doing something an operative would do."*

I am almost out of air. He's not letting go. This is it.
I either die here, or I let CTA control me like a puppet.
Who knows why they really want him dead. I'm sure he
has his reasons for dying, but I'm even more sure that
CTA wants him dead.

More than that, I know I'm not finished. I can't
think like myself anymore. That life is behind me, even
if I'm still a stand-up comedian. I'm somebody new.

I reach out to the knife I dropped on the pavement,
and I plunge it into the guy's neck.

He lets go of my throat and grabs my wrist, trying to
get the knife free. A racking cough rips through my
lungs, but I keep the knife pressed into his skin as hard
as I can. I'm waiting for the blood to fall but it doesn't. I
look at his face, trying to see if he looks ready to pass
out. His face is red, and I realize he is having trouble
breathing, but not because of the wound. He's laughing.

"You actually did it, Drew."

Now I know this guy is nuts. I let go of the knife,
ready to run. Instead of staying in his neck, the knife
falls to the asphalt.

The guy's neck doesn't have a mark on it.

I'm dumbfounded, and my legs refuse to work. I watch as he kneels down. He picks up the knife, presses a finger to it, and then pushes the blade into the handle.

A fake knife.

"Pretty good joke, huh?"

"*Joke?*" I gasp.

"Oh, come on, Drew. You're a comedian, ain't ya?"

Now I'm not dumbfounded. I'm livid. This was all another stupid test. This was supposed to be a real-world mission! I'm starting to think CTA isn't taking me seriously. I don't know what they're waiting for. I've done everything I can to prove I'm serious, and still they think I don't have what it takes. It hurts that Red would trick me like this when she said I was ready. Does she think I'm still that green?

"Take the car, Drew. That's your next step." The guy hands me the keys and walks away before I can say another word.

I don't even look at the car. I know I'm not doing whatever it is the next stop is supposed to be.

I need CTA to know I am all in.

Los Angeles, California

The red eye to Los Angeles did nothing for my nerves. When I decided I couldn't sleep, I drank a cup of coffee that only gave me heart burn. After I landed in LAX, I took less than an hour checking into a low-key hotel room and making my way over here. Now I'm standing outside the building on Wilshire with zero sleep and a massive headache. I wasn't happy before, and I'm sure not happy now.

I was going to stand here and see if looking at the building made me change my mind, but now I'm only more certain that this is what I have to do. I need to prove that I'm serious, and that means I need to see that foie grasshole again and tell him, face to face.

Before I can convince myself not to do it, I open the front door to the building and step inside. The air conditioning is a welcome greeting and makes me realize I was sweating standing outside. I take a minute to collect myself at the elevators as I read off the business names beside the floor numbers. Right near the top floor is Craft Talent Agency. I'm a little surprised they put their name on the plaque when I can only assume they are running their espionage business in this building, but they've gotten this far without anyone questioning them. Maybe they've gotten cocky

Before I step into the elevator, I swear I can feel eyes on my neck. It's the same feeling I had when I spotted the tail back in San Diego. I bend down to tie my already tied shoelace and use a steel trashcan by the elevator doors to see every angle around me. No one.

The elevator doors open, and a group of what look to be interns floods out, probably headed to an early lunch. I take the opportunity to slip into the elevator and smash the door closed button. If somebody is following me, I don't care. That's the point. They think I still need to be tested when I don't.

As I wait for the dozen floors to pass by, I work myself into such a rage that I'm breathing like I did when I ran to meet that old woman. I'm reminded again how much I have been judged during this whole ordeal, and incredibly, that makes me even angrier.

The ding of the elevator doors tells me I've arrived, and I step out into what is obviously an entire floor devoted to CTA. Dozens of employees bustle about, carrying documents, shouting into mouthpieces, and frantically typing into smartphones. I stop the first person who passes by, a flustered young blonde who looks late for a meeting.

"Where is he?"

She stares at me, annoyed. "Where is who?"

I roll my eyes, hoping she will assume I am talking about the suit. I don't actually know his name.

It works. She sighs exasperatedly. "In his office."

I give her a nod and move along. I complete a circuit of the floor and when I come to the last corner, I know I've found it. It's the largest office on the floor by far, and though I can't see through the frosted glass doors, I can see the sunlight shining into the office from what I can only assume are the huge glass windows I saw from the street.

I don't know what I'm going to say. I don't know if I'll even have to say anything. What I do know is that I'm finally doing something instead of just following orders.

Taking a deep breath, I open the doors and charge in.

"Congratulations, Drew. You lose."

It's the suit, as I expected, but standing beside his desk is Red. The eyes on me at the elevator had to have been hers. I can't read discern her emotions at all. She might be disappointed, but she might also be angry or even disgusted. I never got a lesson on reading facial expressions.

The suit raises his hand and moves his index and middle fingers in a come-here motion. I think he's gesturing to me at first, but then two security guards I hadn't noticed at either side of the doors step forward and loop their arms through both of mine.

"What the hell?"

The guards start dragging me out before the suit even responds.

"I came here to prove I was all in!" I shout.

Again, the suit doesn't answer. The goons tug me backwards while I thrash my arms.

"Red! Tell him I'm in."

It's almost imperceptible, but I see a quick flash in her eyes before she moves her gaze away.

Just like that, I'm gone from the office quicker than I'd come in. They escort me all the way through the front doors of the building and dump me on the sidewalk unceremoniously.

Frozen in place, I rake my hands through my hair as they walk back inside. This can't be happening.

I don't know what I'm supposed to do now, but I

need time to think. Maybe if I go back to the motel and give it time, Red will show up in a disguise and tell me I really screwed up this time.

After hailing a cab, I'm still convinced I can fix this. I spend the drive thinking about what I'll tell Red. I don't know if she'll believe any of it. All it boils down to is that I wanted them to know I can handle what they throw at me.

When I slide my credit card to pay for the trip, it's declined. What the hell? I slide it again, and still nothing.

"Something wrong with your machine?" I ask.

"No, sir," the cabby says flatly, still impatiently waiting for some kind of money. I fork over cash so I can get the hell out of his cab and into the hotel.

At my room, the same thing happens. I slide the card, and red lights flash back at me. Unbelievable. I stomp back to the lobby and hand the key card to the receptionist.

"Room 212. Key's not working."

"I'm sorry. I can make you a new one. Do you have your ID?"

I frown because this guy just checked me in an hour ago, but I hand it over anyway. I'm not in the mood to listen to his policy rant.

"You said 212? We don't have anybody staying in 212."

Ordinarily, I would believe that I made a mistake, but not after Red's training. I'm perceptive. I don't miss critical details.

"I'm positive. Can you look it up by my name?"

"Well, that's the trouble. We don't have a Drew Roberts staying here."

Now I'm pissed. "This is ridiculous. All of my stuff is in that room." Then I realize my *cash* is in that room. "You checked me in yourself," I tell him now.

"I'm really sorry, sir. Another guest is listed as being in that room. Are you here with family? Could the room be under their name instead?"

"You know that I wasn't with anyone else."

"I'm so sorry sir, but if your last name doesn't match the one on the reservation, I can't let you in the room."

"What name is on the reservation?"

"I'm not at liberty to disclose that information," he says quietly, knowing this is going to set me off.

I try to play it cool, though, because all that matters to me is my suitcase full of cash. "Look, it doesn't matter. All I want is the suitcase I left in the room. Guests leave items behind all the time. Can you check in the room?"

The guy is nervous now, looking between the phone and the hallway leading to the rooms. Finally, he reaches down and dials a number. "Yes, sir, I'm sorry to trouble you. The guest who stayed in your room previously forgot an item."

"*Multiple* items," I say loudly so whoever stole my room can hear. This is outrageous. It's bad enough CTA dropped me on my ass, and now I'm dealing with this idiocy.

"You're quite sure?"

Heat rises to my face because of course whoever is in that room now would lie if they found my cash. I don't even think about what I'm doing. I book it down the hallway and pound my fist on Room 212's door.

When it opens, a skinny elderly man with coke-bottle glasses looks up at me.

The receptionist has caught up, but the elderly man has already stepped aside to let me through.

"Please, please, come in, come in. It was your room? I'm sure I saw nothing. I always check for bed bugs, and I looked in every corner," he says proudly.

Without a shadow of a doubt, I know this man didn't take my suitcase. I'm an idiot. My card stop didn't stop working. The hotel key card wasn't a coincidence.

This is all CTA's doing.

I apologize to the man and turn to the receptionist. "I need to use the front desk phone."

"Sir, I'm not sure I can do that . . ."

"Look, you know I checked in here, and I know I checked in here. I have no clue what happened to my stuff. The least you can do is let me make a phone call."

His nerves jangle again, but he finally nods, and walks me over to the desk. I quickly dial the only number I have memorized. Todd Rainey.

"Hello?"

"Todd, it's me."

"Who's that?"

"It's Drew. Look, I know I screwed up, and I know

225

you can't fix it for me, but they've left in the trenches here, and I'm—"

"Whoa, whoa, slow down. *Who's* this?"

My back goes cold. "Todd, stop messing with me. I'm stressed enough as it is. I need your help."

"Look, pal, I'm sure you need help, but you've got the wrong guy. I've never met anyone named Drew in my life. Good luck."

The phone clicks.

A sinking feeling spreads in my gut. I can't panic, because that will mean this is really happening. As I dial Todd's number again very carefully, I try to take deep breaths, but it isn't helping. I hit the final number and press the phone to my ear.

"The number you are trying to call is not reachable."

The phone doesn't make it back on the hook. It falls from my grasp and clatters onto the desk. Distantly, I see the receptionist hang it up.

They took everything from me. My money. My agent. Without contacting Duffy, I know the tour is over, too. They've stripped me of everything—even what I had before I let Duffy convince me to do this. I'm all alone. I'm a nobody.

What the hell do I do now?

"You know," the receptionist says, "I didn't think you were him at first, but now I think you might just be."

"Might just be who?"

"A woman came in. Said to give this to a frenzied-looking hobo."

My jaw drops. *Hobo?*

"You looked frenzied, but not like a hobo." He lifts a yellow piece of paper from his desk but doesn't hand it to me yet.

My heart wants it to be what I know it can't. I ask anyway. "What'd she look like? Old? Young? Blonde? Red-head?"

"Don't know. Could barely see her face. But her eyes, man. They were the exact color of—"

"Jade," I say before he can. Somehow managing not to fall on the floor in relief, I reach out for the paper. As I take the folded Post-it, I concentrate on keeping my fingers from shaking. After opening it up, I see two words that give me a flutter of hope.

FIND ME

ACKNOWLEDGMENTS

This book was long in the making. Thank you to every human who had to listen to me saying, "I should finish my book." There are too many of you to name.

Thank you to my family, which will guarantee I sell at least three books.

Thank you to my team: my manager, Peter Rosegarten, Joel Zimmer, and Ruth Mcgary. You have always been my sounding board.

But mostly, I thank everyone who has ever come to one of my shows, or has bought or streamed my albums. Thank you so much.

ABOUT THE AUTHOR

John Heffron is a stand-up comedian and winner of the second season of NBC's *Last Comic Standing*. He has performed for thirty years, appearing on *The Tonight Show*, *The Late Late Show*, *WTF with Marc Maron*, *The Joe Rogan Experience*, *Brad Paisley's Comedy Rodeo*, *Chelsea Lately*, and *Ari Shaffir's Skeptic Tank*.

Heffron has released five comedy albums (*The Laughs You Deserve*; *Episodes*; *The Better Half*; *Good Kid, Bad Adult*; and *The Kid with a Cape*), the comedy special *Middle Class Funny*, and is coauthor with Topher Morrison of *I Come to You from the Future: Everything You'll Need to Know before You Know It*.

In addition to headlining clubs and appearing at festivals around the world, Heffron is available for corporate bookings. You can find his tour dates and booking information at www.johnheffron.com, and you can stream his albums wherever you listen to music.

Made in the USA
Monee, IL
13 July 2020

35829222R00142